NO RIGHT TO KILL

DI SARA RAMSEY BOOK 1

M A COMLEY

JEAMEL PUBLISHING LIMITED

ACKNOWLEDGMENTS

Thank you as always to my rock, Jean, I'd be lost without you in my life.

Special thanks to Studioenp for creating such a superb cover.

My heartfelt thanks go to my wonderful editor Emmy Ellis @ Studioenp and to my fabulous proofreader Joseph Calleja for spotting all the lingering nits.

And finally, thank you to all the members of my wonderful ARC group for coming on this special journey with me and helping me to grow as an author. Love you all.

New York Times and USA Today bestselling author M A Comley

Published by Jeamel Publishing limited

Copyright © 2018 M A Comley

Digital Edition, License Notes

ALSO BY M A COMLEY

Blind Justice (Novella)

Cruel Justice (Book #1)

Mortal Justice (Novella)

Impeding Justice (Book #2)

Final Justice (Book #3)

Foul Justice (Book #4)

Guaranteed Justice (Book #5)

Ultimate Justice (Book #6)

Virtual Justice (Book #7)

Hostile Justice (Book #8)

Tortured Justice (Book #9)

Rough Justice (Book #10)

Dubious Justice (Book #11)

Calculated Justice (Book #12)

Twisted Justice (Book #13)

Justice at Christmas (Short Story)

Prime Justice (Book #14)

Heroic Justice (Book #15)

Shameful Justice (Book #16)

Immoral Justice (Book #17)

Toxic Justice (Book #18 coming Dec 2018)

Unfair Justice (a 10,000 word short story)

Irrational Justice (a 10,000 word short story)

Seeking Justice (a 15,000 word novella)

Clever Deception (co-written by Linda S Prather)

Tragic Deception (co-written by Linda S Prather)

Sinful Deception (co-written by Linda S Prather)

NO Right To Kill (DI Sara Ramsey Book 1)

Forever Watching You (DI Miranda Carr thriller)

Wrong Place (DI Sally Parker thriller #1)

No Hiding Place (DI Sally Parker thriller #2)

Cold Case (DI Sally Parker thriller#3)

Deadly Encounter (DI Sally Parker thriller #4)

Lost Innocence (DI Sally Parker thriller #5)

Web of Deceit (DI Sally Parker Novella with Tara Lyons)

The Missing Children (DI Kayli Bright #1)

Killer On The Run (DI Kayli Bright #2)

Hidden Agenda (DI Kayli Bright #3)

Murderous Betrayal (Kayli Bright #4)

Dying Breath (Kayli Bright #5)

The Hostage Takers (DI Kayli Bright Novella)

The Caller (co-written with Tara Lyons)

Evil In Disguise – a novel based on True events

Deadly Act (Hero series novella)

Torn Apart (Hero series #1)

End Result (Hero series #2)

In Plain Sight (Hero Series #3)

Double Jeopardy (Hero Series #4)

Sole Intention (Intention series #1)

Grave Intention (Intention series #2)

Devious Intention (Intention #3)

Merry Widow (A Lorne Simpkins short story)

It's A Dog's Life (A Lorne Simpkins short story)

A Time To Heal (A Sweet Romance)

A Time For Change (A Sweet Romance)

High Spirits

The Temptation series (Romantic Suspense/New Adult Novellas)

Past Temptation

Lost Temptation

PROLOGUE

Time is a cruel thief to rob us of our former selves. We lose as much to life as we do to death.

Elizabeth Forsythe Hailey

He watched the house, waiting…

In the safety of his car, he reflected. Wondering if he had the courage to pull this off. To carry out what he was planning to do to the old couple who had befriended him. Shown him love when others had all too often turned their backs on him. Sweat broke out on his forehead, and his hands became clammy. He'd thought long and hard about doing this, so why was he having doubts now?

The light went on at the other end of the bungalow. He knew the inside of the home well—someone had gone into the bedroom. Should he strike now? Or wait until the couple had gone to bed?

He decided to leave it a little while. It was only ten o'clock. His stomach clenched and tied itself into knots. Again, he debated whether he was doing the right thing as the elderly couple's smiling faces entered his mind.

They had celebrated their sixtieth wedding anniversary only the year before. Welcomed him along with all their family and friends in the small village to join in the fun. Sixty years spent together was such an amazing achievement these days.

Swallowing hard, he shook his head. *I can't do this! Not to them.* But he *had* to. He'd run out of options. His mind drifted back to the party the family had held in their honour, how much everyone cherished them. The couple had been childhood sweethearts, only ever had eyes for each other, a rarity in this day and age.

Why had he overheard Ted spouting his mouth off down at the pub? That's what this was all about. His desire to have what the couple were hiding in their home. Ted had repeatedly told his friend, whilst sitting at the bar, how much he detested banks, even went as far as to call them thieving bastards—he found it hard to trust them enough to look after his money.

With his heart pounding, he wiped drool away with the sleeve of his jacket. Money was an excellent motivator for people without much to celebrate in their lives. He worked hard when he was employed. All right, he always messed up and got the sack regularly, but when he was at work, he'd enjoyed the camaraderie he'd shared with his workmates. The trouble was, that lately he spent more time out of work than in employment. Any money he had went on the necessities in life, like keeping a roof over his head and paying the bills. There was never enough to go around to spend on things that put happiness in his heart.

Inhaling a large breath, he plucked up the courage to leave his car. He scanned the area quickly, closed the door softly behind him and dashed across the road, the outside light of the house acting as a beacon, enticing him closer.

Once he reached the porch, he took a final glance around and then rang the bell. Moments later, Ted opened the door and seemed genuinely pleased to see him.

He almost turned back and walked away, but the lure of what was waiting for him inside proved impossible for him to ignore.

Ted stepped back, inviting him into his home, the way he always did. Guilt wrapped itself around his heart. He had to push that aside and concentrate on making his goals achievable. He had a vast debt to pay. That was why he was doing this, no other reason. He thought of Ted and Maureen as members of his family. But if he didn't do this, *his* life would be on the line.

Killing them would mean his own salvation…

CHAPTER 1

Always punctual, Detective Inspector Sara Ramsey arrived at work half an hour before her shift was due to begin. She was surprised to find her partner, Detective Sergeant Carla Jameson, already working at her desk.

"Blimey! Did you shit the bed or something?"

Carla's dainty nose wrinkled. "Crap, you can be so uncouth at times, boss."

Sara laughed. "I'll consider myself reprimanded with that remark. What are you up to?"

"Tying up a few loose ends. You know me, hate it when I'm drowning in paperwork. Makes it hard to concentrate when another case drops on my desk."

"I admire your conscientiousness. Wish everyone on the team possessed the same work ethic. Sadly, that's not the case. Anything on the wires overnight?" Sara asked on her way to the vending machine. She returned with two cups of coffee and placed one on the desk next to Carla.

"Thanks. All quiet as far as I can tell. Mind you, I last viewed the computer an hour ago. A mass murderer could have struck in that time."

Sara shook her head and tutted. "Hardly. Not on our patch. Nothing that gritty happens in sleepy Herefordshire, in case you hadn't noticed."

Carla's eyebrows rose. "I think you're forgetting the masked hold-up at the bank we had recently. Plus, the incident concerning the man who deliberately ran down his wife because she was seeking a divorce."

She raised her hands in defeat. "All right, maybe those couple of incidents slipped my mind. Anyway, an hour, you said. What time did you get here this morning?"

"Around seven. Andrew had a meeting in London and needed to get on the road by six. You know what I'm like. Once I'm awake, that's it for the day. Thought I'd be better off coming in early."

"What was the alternative?"

Carla shrugged. "An early morning run or tidying up the house, neither of which appealed to me at six this morning. The only other option left open to me was to start work early." She took a sip from her coffee and pulled a face. "Crap, you forgot the sugar." She opened the drawer beside her and withdrew a packet of granulated sugar and a teaspoon.

"No, I didn't. I ordered one sugar as usual," Sara objected adamantly.

"The damn machine must have run out again. I keep telling Will and Barry to stop filling their coffee with five sugars, selfish shits!"

Sara tasted her own coffee and shuddered. "Stick one in there for me. I'll need to ring the vending machine people, ask them to top it up again."

"You'd be better off telling the boys to buy their own bag of sugar."

"I'll do that as well. Right, I'll be in my office should you need me. There's bound to be a mountain of paperwork vying for my attention after the weekend."

"Crampons at the ready. I poked my head in the office earlier, on the off-chance you were in."

Curling her lip, Sara rolled her eyes up to the ceiling and walked across the incident room to her office. The office overlooked the park opposite. Every morning, Sara passed the first few minutes of her day gazing out the window at the green open space opposite and the view of the Brecon Beacons in the distance. She hadn't been in the area long, but she already considered it her home. She'd transferred from Liverpool—a tough patch to patrol—to possibly one of the most laid-back areas an inspector could wish to work in. Her eyes misted up when she thought about the real reason she'd come south. After what had happened, she realised how much she missed her family.

Her mother and father had been a tower of strength to her in the past eighteen months since she'd landed on their doorstep. But after years of independence, she had found it difficult to live under someone else's roof, abiding by their rules. A developer was constructing a new-build site of twenty houses in the village next to her parents', so she'd jumped at the chance of putting down a deposit on one of the first houses that had been erected on the site.

Her parents had been a little disappointed when she'd first told them of her plans, but after a few frosty days, they'd finally given their blessing. Sara had moved into her two-bedroom house only a few months ago with Misty, her tortoiseshell cat.

She left the window and slipped behind her desk to finish her coffee. *There's no point in me getting all maudlin. That won't bring him back.* She was where she belonged, returned to the family fold now. Living in this area was a whole world away from the life she'd had in Liverpool. Her parents were now enjoying their retirement, safe in the knowledge that she no longer served in a force with a substantial crime rate that was increasing year on year.

The only downside to her parents' retirement plans was that her father had an ongoing problem with his heart that the specialist at the hospital was keeping a regular eye on. Other than that, she was enjoying working in Hereford and living close to her family, even if the godawful memories reared their head now and again.

Sara glanced up from her paperwork when Carla opened the door. "You spoke too soon."

She tilted her head and frowned. "I did? About what?"

"About nothing juicy ever happening around here. Looks like we have a double murder on our patch."

Sara collapsed against the back of her chair. "What?" she said in disbelief. "You're kidding me?"

Carla's mouth turned down, and she shook her head slowly. "I wish I was. An elderly couple stabbed to death in their home."

"Shit! Okay. Get the details, and we'll shoot over there now. I take it the pathologist is already at the scene?"

"She is, along with her team."

"Give me five minutes to at least finish opening the post, and I'll be with you. Is anyone else in yet?"

Carla glanced at her watch. "Nope, but they shouldn't be long, it's eight-fifty."

"We'll get on the road once someone else arrives. You know how much I detest leaving the phones unmanned."

Carla left the room. Sara tried not to dwell on the crime too much as she completed her first task of the morning. With that out of the way, she left her desk, slipped on her jacket and joined the rest of the team in the incident room. "Morning all. I take it Carla has brought you up to date? We're going to take a ride over there, to see the crime scene for ourselves."

"Morning, boss. Anything in particular you want us to tackle in your absence?" asked DS Will Rogerson.

"Why don't you start the background checks on the couple? Carla will give you the details before we leave."

Will left his chair and wandered over to Carla's desk where she scribbled down the information for him. Once Carla had handed over the sheet of paper, Sara said, "Are we ready to rumble, partner?"

Carla unhooked her jacket from the chair, drank the rest of her coffee and nodded. "All ready."

"See you later, guys," Sara called over her shoulder as they made their way through the swing doors.

"Crap, it's only just registered with me. I only live a few villages away, so do my parents," Sara said, halting the car outside the victims' bungalow in Bodenham.

"This is probably a one-off. No point getting yourself worked up about it."

Sara raised an eyebrow at her partner. "I hope you're bloody right on that one. Otherwise I'm going to get it in the neck from my parents."

"Why?"

"I can just imagine the conversation now. 'We never had these types of crimes in our area before you moved down here!'"

Carla laughed. "I think all parents would say that in this case, not just yours."

They exited the car and prepared to show their IDs to the uniformed officer standing close to the cordon. "DI Sara Ramsey and DS Carla Jameson."

The young male officer hoisted up the tape, enabling them both to duck under it.

"Is the pathologist inside?"

"Yes, ma'am."

Walking up the winding path to the bungalow, Sara couldn't help but admire how beautifully manicured the lawn was and how tidy the borders of the front garden were. The property was detached, surrounded by its own grounds with a single garage at the side with what Sara presumed was the couple's car, a maroon-coloured Ford, sitting in the drive. "Nicely tended garden."

"Yep. I thought the same. The couple obviously cherished it," Carla agreed.

Sara opened the front door and called out, "Hello, anyone in here?"

"Do not come in here until you're togged up, got that?"

Sara recognised the voice of Lorraine Dixon, the local pathologist.

"Can we nick some suits from your car, Lorraine?"

A groan was quickly followed by a brief *yes*.

Sara and Carla returned to the parked cars and located the pathologist's right away. They extracted two white paper suits, pulled them on, and then slipped a pair of blue paper shoes over their feet. Prepared for what lay ahead, they retraced their steps and entered the house. They found Lorraine standing in the lounge, also dressed for the occasion, having a discussion with her team. She turned to face Sara and Carla and motioned for them to join her.

Lorraine seemed despondent. "It's a mess."

"Where are the bodies?" Sara asked, her gaze latching on to two big pools of blood on the carpet close to where Lorraine was standing. A familiar feeling of wanting to shut out the world and curl up in a ball swept over her, but she quickly brushed it aside.

Lorraine pointed behind Sara. "Down the hallway, in the bedroom."

"The killer moved the bodies?"

"Seems to be the case. No idea why just yet. Also, we haven't spotted any sign of forced entry," Lorraine concurred.

"Interesting. A savage attack all the same. Who found them?"

Lorraine pointed out the window. "The woman sitting in the black Vectra. She's the couple's daughter."

"Damn! That must have been tough for her. I'll have a word with her in a minute. Do you want to walk me through the scene?"

Lorraine nodded. "Not been here that long myself, therefore I haven't managed to figure out the whys and wherefores just yet. All I can tell you at this point is that the murders took place here, and the assailant, or assailants, moved the bodies to the rear of the property."

Sara surveyed the room and pointed at the large bay window. "Maybe the killer thought the bodies would be on view if anyone peered in."

"That was my first thought. The net curtain doesn't reach the windowsill—maybe they assumed someone would peer underneath."

"I think you're right. Giving them time to abscond without the fear of getting caught."

"Maybe. Heartless nevertheless. Do we know how old the victims were?"

Lorraine sighed. "Rough guesstimate, I would put them in their late seventies to early eighties."

Sara flung her arms out to the sides in frustration. "Why? Who would do such a thing to people of that age? It's sickening." Her heart skipped several beats when her own grandparents' faces filtered into her mind. They had both been frail at that age, hardly able to put up a fight to save their lives.

"I don't think anyone in this room is going to disagree with you on that point. Shall we go through to the bedroom? Avoid stepping in the trail of blood en route, if you will?" Lorraine walked ahead of Sara and Carla. She entered the room and steered around the two dead bodies lying on the floor close to the bed.

The three of them remained silent for a few moments, observing the scene.

Finally, Sara shook her head and groaned. "Sick beyond words. Such a vicious attack, and yet the place doesn't appear to have been ransacked. Why? Why kill them?"

"Your guess is as good as mine and non-existent at this point, Inspector," Lorraine confirmed.

"Do you think the murderer knew them?" Carla asked, still transfixed by the bodies.

"Who knows?" Lorraine replied.

Sara leaned over to study the couple closer and asked, "Why is the man's body twisted like that?"

Lorraine shrugged. "Maybe the killer was searching for something, a wallet or driving licence perhaps."

Sara sighed and stood up again. "You might be right. His back pocket is on view. I know my father keeps his wallet in his at all times."

"Agreed. I'm looking at how many stab wounds there are," Carla said. "It would seem to be a frenzied attack, as if the assailant knew them personally. Or am I reading too much into it?"

Lorraine and Sara glanced at each other and nodded their agreement. "Possibly. That's usually the way these things turn out," Lorraine agreed.

"Should make it easier to solve in that case," Carla suggested.

Sara wasn't so sure. In her experience, murderers never actually fit into set categories just because of the way they slaughtered their victims. "Let's keep that thought on the back burner for now."

"Not always," Lorraine said. "Early days yet, but so far it seems the killer was careful not to leave any DNA. However, in the hallway I spotted a trainer print in the blood."

"That's excellent news, isn't it?" Sara asked, perplexed by the concerned expression on the pathologist's face.

"It would be if the print was irregular in some way. Sadly, it isn't."

Sara tutted. "That's a shame. You'll still examine it and report back, right?"

"Of course. There's really nothing else I can tell you at this moment in time. Now, if you'll excuse me, I need to organise the team properly."

"Sorry. If we have any more questions, I'll come and grab you." Sara smiled at the pathologist.

After Lorraine had left the room, Sara surveyed the scene, avoiding looking at the victims for now. "Okay, I'm going to suggest what happened here. Speak up if you think I'm wrong. The woman was in bed, probably reading her book. There's a cup on the bedside table and biscuit crumbs in the bed, plus she's in her nightdress. Maybe she heard the doorbell ring and put her dressing gown on to investigate who the caller was."

"You got all that just from a few clues?" Carla asked, showing her inexperience in dealing with a murder case.

"You need to take in the bigger picture, partner. Don't stop at the obvious clues that are presented to you. Go beyond that. Did you notice the broken vase in the lounge?"

Carla shook her head. "No. Not that we were in the room long enough."

"Well, it was there. My guess is that the woman went to investigate who the caller was and found the person, or persons, attacking her husband. She probably bashed them with the vase trying to save her husband. Most women would scream for help and try to run out of the house. I don't think that happened in this case. She loved the bones of this man. They had probably spent their whole life together. More than likely she would think she'd be better off dead than live the rest of her life in misery without her husband, therefore she put up a decent fight. Look at the stab wounds she received, dozens of them."

"Shocking. Can't believe someone would possess that much hatred to take out an elderly couple in such a horrendous way," Carla said, her gaze dropping back to the couple.

"We need to get past our personal feelings on this, Carla, and quickly. Experience tells me that if the assailant or assailants got what they were after, they'll get a thirst to kill and brutalise more people."

"No. I hope you're wrong on that count. Things like this just don't occur around here."

Sara tilted her head and pointed at the victims. "Evidently they do." She moved over to the window. "This place isn't overlooked as such."

"It's still worth checking with the neighbours to see if they saw or heard anything though, right?"

Sara faced her partner. "No doubt about that. Do you want to start the enquiries while I speak to the daughter? I think we've left her alone long enough, don't you?"

"Agreed. I'll do the rounds and report back if anything grabs my attention."

Sara and Carla rejoined Lorraine in the lounge. On the way, Sara noted all the family photos lining the wall. The couple always had a smile on their faces. *Heartbreaking! Mindless, selfish behaviour on the killer's part, no doubt.* "We'll be back once we've spoken to the daughter and the neighbours; we're not running off just yet."

"Very well. We'll continue to process the scene."

They left the house and split up at the garden gate. Carla went left to the neighbour's property while Sara walked over to the Vectra parked on the opposite side of the road. The driver had her head resting on the steering wheel. Sara was concerned that if she tapped on the window she'd scare the woman. She approached the driver's side and opened the door.

The woman immediately sat back in her seat and turned to look at Sara. Her face was blotchy, and trails of mascara stained her cheeks.

"Hello. I'm DI Sara Ramsey. I'm so sorry for your loss. Would it be all right if I jump in and have a chat with you?"

"I'm Olivia Morgan." She reached for a handy pack of tissues in the console and extracted one. After wiping her eyes and blowing her nose, she nodded. "Please, yes, get in."

Sara walked around the front of the car and slotted into the passenger seat. She swivelled to face the woman. "Are you up to telling me how you discovered your parents?"

"I came by as planned this morning. Mum had a hospital appointment in Hereford, a glaucoma check-up. I promised I would go with her."

"I see. Can I ask when you last spoke to either your father or your mother?"

"Saturday evening, around eight o'clock." Olivia sniffled and slammed her hand onto the steering wheel. "They celebrated their sixtieth anniversary last year. Forty years they've lived in this property. How could anyone do this to them? Why would anyone want to hurt my parents, let alone *kill* them?"

Sara swallowed down the feeling of helplessness she usually felt at times like this. The inability to answer distraught families during such emotional times was the one side of her job that truly let her down. "I'm sorry, I just can't answer your questions right now. Not until the investigation has begun properly."

"You must have some indication who could do this? Didn't they leave any clues behind? DNA for instance?"

"The pathologist and her team are in there now. If there is any evidence to be found, they'll find it, I assure you."

"Didn't the neighbours hear anything? Surely someone must have heard a scream or shout. I doubt Mum would have gone quietly," Olivia said, fresh tears falling onto her cheeks.

"My partner is doing the rounds with the neighbours now. Hopefully she'll have some good news for us soon."

"My next question would be, if someone did hear a scream, then why didn't they call the police?"

"That would be my first question, too. Let's wait and see what develops first. Do you know the neighbours well?"

She sniffled and wiped her nose. "Most of them have lived alongside my parents for years. I'm sure they would have assisted them if they'd known they were in trouble. Oh, I don't know. Who knows how people will react if confronted with something as terrible as this? You hear of so many violent crimes being committed on our streets in the big cities such as London and Birmingham, but not out in the sticks, for Christ's sake. I'm appalled this should happen. My parents were churchgoers, never spoke badly of anyone. Why? Why would someone go out of their way to kill them?"

Sara's throat clogged up when Olivia broke down again. She reached over and patted the woman's hand. "Please try not to upset yourself further. I promise you we'll get to the bottom of this. Find the person responsible. However, we'll need your help to do that. I know that's not what you want to hear at this stage, but we need to find out what this person's motives were. There are signs that this person, or persons, were known to your parents."

Olivia turned to face her, her eyes wide with surprise. "What? How do you know that?"

"I'm surmising that's the case. The pathologist informed me that there is no sign of a forced entry. Taking that into consideration, I would suggest that whoever opened the door to the killer, knew them and invited them into the house."

Olivia narrowed her eyes as she contemplated the scenario. "Actually, you're probably right. My parents were pretty hot on security. All right, they didn't possess any CCTV cameras, never felt the need to have them living in a rural idyll such as this, but how does someone prepare for every eventuality? Even something as brutal as this?"

"Okay, that reinforces what I thought. Can you think of anyone you know who would have a vendetta against your parents?"

Adamantly shaking her head, Olivia replied, "No, no one. They were both well loved in the community, and all their family adored them."

Sara blew out a frustrated breath. "I have to ask in that case if your parents kept any valuables in the house. Whoever killed them were after something specific. By the looks of things, the house wasn't turned over at all, and their car is still parked in the drive. Did they have anything else of value that someone could possibly be after?"

Inhaling a shuddering breath, Olivia nodded. "My father didn't trust banks. He hated what they stood for and refused to deposit any money with them."

Sara's interest piqued. "Did your parents have a safe in the house?"

"No. Dad always kept the money under a floorboard in the bedroom, under the bed."

Reflecting on the way Olivia's father's body was positioned, Sara asked, "Where did your father keep his wallet?"

"In his back pocket. He always kept five hundred pounds in it, for emergencies."

"Okay. The pathologist presumed your father had been turned over to gain access to his back pocket, which is now empty."

"That's the motive then?" Olivia asked, her brow knitted.

"Possibly," Sara admitted.

"Where do we go from here? I've been sitting here, too stunned to ring my family to tell them. They're going to be devastated beyond belief that this could happen in this sleepy village. Why would anyone carry out such a heinous crime in the middle of nowhere?"

"That's what I intend to find out, and believe me when I say this, Mrs Morgan. I will find out."

Olivia sighed and reached for her mobile phone. "Thank you, that's reassuring. I'm going to ring my brothers now."

"I don't envy you that task. I will need their addresses after you ring them. To interview them in case they can fill in any of the blanks we have at present, if you wouldn't mind pre-warning them."

"Of course. I hope they'll be able to help you more than I have."

Sara placed a hand on Olivia's forearm. "You've done your best in the circumstances. I'll leave you a card just in case anything comes to mind that you think we should be aware of in the next few days. Again, I'm very sorry for your loss."

"Thank you. I hope you can furnish us with the justice we seek, Inspector."

"I hope so, too. I'll leave you to make the calls and speak to you again before we leave." Sara exited the car on shaky legs. Carla was coming out of one of the neighbours' houses in front of her. "Anything of use?"

"Sort of. The lady, a Mavis Nicholl, told me that she thought she heard a scream around tennish on Saturday night. She immediately left her home and knocked on the Flowers' door. But no one answered. She presumed she had imagined it and returned to her house and didn't think any more of it."

"She didn't bother to check the following day in the daylight? Were the lights still on in the house on the Saturday night?"

"She said the place was in darkness and she didn't call round there yesterday because her family came to pick her up at nine and she was out all day with them for some kind of family party."

"Great. Okay, maybe she knocked on the door and disturbed the intruder. Perhaps Mrs Flowers screamed, and her assailant swiftly killed her then switched off the lights on the assumption that one of the neighbours might come knocking to investigate." She scanned the other houses within spitting distance of where they stood. "Have you had a chance to speak to any of the others yet?"

"Not yet. Mrs Nicholl kept me talking a while. I think she's scared, she lives alone."

"That's to be expected. We need to reassure anyone else we speak to that this type of thing is a rarity and that we'll be keeping an eye on the area. I'll organise a patrol car to drive by a few times every day, just to give the neighbours some peace of mind."

"Good idea. How was the daughter?"

"Surprisingly calm in the circumstances. Maybe she'd had a chance to get her head around what had happened while she waited for the pathologist to show up. I've left her ringing the other members of the family. I'll check back on her in a while. Let's split up and continue the door-to-door enquiries."

Carla nodded and entered the next garden to her left while Sara walked across the road to a smart-looking bungalow with a garden brimming full of cottage plants, most of which were in full bloom. She rang the doorbell and waited, feeling a little perkier on the inside as she observed the beautiful plants surrounding her. She was always on the lookout for ideas of how to make her tiny patch of garden bright and cheerful. She didn't have a clue what it would take to achieve something of this standard, but it didn't stop her appreciating how wonderful the display was.

An elderly man opened the door, his reading glasses perched on the end of his nose. His gaze drifted behind Sara, at the official vehicles beyond his gate.

"Hello, sir." Sara held up her ID for him to see. "I'm DI Sara Ramsey. I wondered if you could spare me a moment to chat."

He seemed dazed, unable to give her his full attention. "I'm sorry. I know nothing. I'm in shock right now."

"I appreciate how traumatic this must be for the community. We're desperately trying to find out how this happened. Is there anything you can tell us? No matter how incidental you believe it to be. Did you happen to see anyone approach the house?" Sara glanced over her shoulder. "I'm thinking your house would have the best view of the Flowers' property."

"It does. I'm sorry I can't be of help, truly I am. They were very dear friends of mine. Ted and I used to go fishing together regularly at the lakes down at Stretton Sugwas. I'll miss him dearly. Shocking it is. To think someone could break into their home and kill them like that. What on earth is this world coming to? Your lot should be back walking the streets. Put the bobbies back in the heart of the communities. It was surprising what we used to detect being able to walk amongst the residents."

"You were a serving officer, I take it, sir?"

"Thirty years I served on the streets of Hereford. It's changed dramatically over the past few years since the regeneration has taken place in the town. Maybe that has something to do with the crime rate going up. What's your take on that, Inspector?"

"I've only recently moved to the area, sir. Can't say I've noticed the crime rate figures have risen to that extent. Maybe you can tell me if you've seen anyone hanging around lately. Someone new to the area or who was acting suspicious, that sort of thing."

"Not really, no." He fell silent, and his eyes screwed up as if he was thinking over her questions in more depth. "Wait a minute. I put the cat out about nine o'clock and noticed an unfamiliar car sitting in the road. Where that SOCO van is now. Didn't think anything more about it until just now—you jogged my memory. Put that down to my old age. I'll be eighty-five in September. The brain is slowing down a touch, getting rusty in places. That's why I like to read, you see, to keep the brain active and sharp."

Her hopes rose a little. "Can you tell me what type of car it was?"

"I only caught a glimpse of it really. A dark car, that's about all I can give you. Never really been bothered about keeping up to date with the vehicle industry. I still drive around in an old Ford Anglia. She's a collector's piece now. Whenever Ted and I went fishing, he always insisted we go in his car. I only tend to go out shopping once a month, you see. I nip down to the local shop in the village if I run out of the essentials in between the major monthly shop."

"I see. Was it dark blue or black?" Sara pressed, not willing to leave it there.

"If push came to shove, I would come down on saying it was black. Sorry I can't give you more than that just now. Maybe something else will register in a day or two. You'll leave me a card in case, right?"

"I will. I don't suppose you could make out who the driver was?"

"No. I didn't think anything of it at the time to be honest with you. In the circumstances, I regret my actions."

"Please, don't feel guilty." Sara handed him a card and turned to look at his garden once more. "You have a fabulous garden. Does it take much to care for it?"

"I'm out here most days pottering around. The back garden is even better. Want me to show you?"

Sara smiled at the old man. "Maybe another time, sir. I better get on and speak to the rest of the neighbours. It was a pleasure meeting you. Don't hesitate to ring me if anything comes to mind."

"I'll do that. Good luck with your investigation. I hope you won't forget about us once you leave here."

"We won't. I'll organise a squad car to drop by every few hours to reassure you and your neighbours."

"Are you sure you can afford such extravagance with your resources these days?"

Sara detected a note of sarcasm in the man's tone. "Yes, sir. I'm sure. Thank you for seeing me. Keep up the excellent work with your garden."

"I will. Good luck with your endeavours."

Sara smiled and walked back up the path, stopping to smell one of the red roses begging for her to appreciate its scent.

"One of my personal favourites. That's a hybrid tea rose called Firefighter."

"Crikey, you can name all the plants as well? You're amazing."

The man sniggered. "Not that amazing, otherwise I would have been able to give you more details about the man sitting in that damn car."

"Maybe something will come to mind soon. Ring me if it does. Goodbye, sir."

The man shut the door. It was then that Sara realised she hadn't taken down his name. She trotted back up the path and rang the bell again.

He opened it, his forehead creased. "Did you forget something?"

"I was so distracted by your wondrous display that I totally forgot to take your name, sir."

"It's Frank Gordon."

"Thank you." Sara turned swiftly to hide her embarrassment. *Get a grip, girl.* Maybe the case was affecting her more than she was willing to admit. Patches of blood had a habit of doing that—at least it had during her time in Liverpool. Another reason she'd decided to leave the area.

She met up with Carla again and asked, "What have you got?"

"Nothing much to go on. The owner of the house said he thought he saw a man approach the house around tennish, give or take a quarter of an hour. He didn't think anything of it because the Flowers had frequent visitors," Carla informed her.

"Could he give you a description?" Sara asked, crossing her fingers down at her side.

"Not really. Youngish, possibly in his twenties or thirties. Pretty vague really."

"That's a damn shame. The neighbour across the road saw a black vehicle parked where the SOCO van is. However, he didn't see who was driving it."

"What time was that?"

"Around nine o'clock."

Carla's mouth twisted. "You reckon he sat there for an hour or so before entering the house?"

"As strange as that sounds, yes. That's exactly what I'm thinking."

"Would a burglar taking a chance on a property really do that?"

"Nope. Which goes back to the point I made in the house that the killer was probably known to the victims. How else would he have gained entry to the property otherwise? Lorraine said there was no evidence of a break-in."

"A family member?" Carla suggested.

Sara shrugged. "Maybe. Who knows at this stage? Let's continue questioning the neighbours. I'll do one more then see how Olivia is getting on with contacting her family."

They split up again, and each ventured down the drive of one of the next two houses. Sara spoke to an elderly woman who was shaking from head to toe as she opened the door. When she introduced herself, the woman broke down in tears, and Sara ended up volunteering to make the woman a cup of strong tea before she left the house empty-handed. Then she went back to see how Olivia was getting on.

Olivia watched her approach the car. She was still on the phone. Sara slowed her pace until she had completed her difficult call. Olivia got out of her car and inhaled a large breath of fresh air. "I've managed to contact all my brothers now. The last one was in an important meeting at work."

"Stupid question: how did they take the news?"

"They were all devastated. David, the last one I spoke to, was livid and wanted to come down here right away. I persuaded him not to. Said there was very little point in him coming as you probably wouldn't allow him access to the house anyway."

"That's true. I'm sorry you had to deal with that alone. How are you holding up?"

Olivia hitched up a shoulder. "I'm all right, I suppose. I've accepted that I'll never see them again and I'm determined to find out why anyone would do this to them."

"As am I. My partner and I have spoken to the neighbours. One of them said she heard a scream and even knocked on the front door but returned to her house and didn't think any more of it when there was no answer."

"Why didn't she ring the police?"

"She thought she had misheard the scream. Said the house was in darkness when she arrived around tennish."

"Didn't she bother to chase it up the next day?"

Sara shook her head. "She was out all day on a family function and never thought to call in to see your parents when she arrived home. She's beside herself, riddled with guilt."

"Now she knows how I feel. I can't shake off the feeling of help-lessness I'm burdened with. When I was telling my brothers, all I could think about was why I hadn't rung them on Sunday."

"Did you usually ring them every day?"

"Not really. I rang on the Saturday evening, then knew I was coming over today to pick Mum up, so I left it."

"You mustn't blame yourself, Olivia. I'm sure dozens of people in your shoes would do the same, but there really is no need."

She sniffled and wiped her nose on a fresh hanky. "So no one saw anything of use to your investigation?"

"We have a sighting of a car sitting outside the property for approx-imately an hour, a dark car, possibly black. Another neighbour said he saw a man approaching the house."

"That's good. Could he describe this man?"

"No. He said your mother and father had that many visitors, he presumed it was a member of your family and didn't think twice about it."

She rubbed a hand over her face. "It's true. There's always one of us popping in and out of here. Damn, do you think it's because all the neighbours are elderly?"

"I don't think so. In my experience, sometimes older witnesses have an advantage over younger ones in that they tend to observe things more thoroughly. Have more time on their hands, if you like."

Olivia glanced at a forensic technician as he left the house and placed an evidence bag in the back of his van. "How long do you think they'll take to examine the house thoroughly? Can I ask why Mum and Dad haven't been taken away yet?"

Sara scratched the side of her face. "It might take them a day or two to carry out an extensive search. I'm sure you appreciate how important it is not to rush these things. I'll have a word with the pathologist to see what's going on with regards to your parents. I'll be right back."

"Thank you. I'd appreciate that, Inspector. The thought of them lying there…well, it's just not right, is it?"

"I agree. Leave it with me." Sara rushed back to the crime scene. Rather than get togged up again, she stuck her head around the door and asked Lorraine, "Not wishing to rush you, but the daughter would like to know when her parents are going to be taken away?"

"I'm organising that now. Sorry for the delay. Given the way the bodies were arranged, I wanted to ensure all the necessary tests and photos were taken first."

"No need to apologise. Anything new for me?" she asked, more out of hope than anticipation.

"Nothing other than what I've shared with you so far."

"One thing the daughter mentioned in passing was her parents kept a vast sum of money under the floorboards beneath the bed. Could one of your guys quickly check that out for me rather than me togging up again?"

"Of course. Paul, would you do the honours for me?"

"On my way now," the young technician said, leaving the room.

"How have the door-to-door enquiries gone?"

Sara tilted her head from side to side. "Nothing spectacular. A few leads to follow up on, though. Send me the results of the PM when you can, as usual."

"You'll be at the top of the list, never worry about that. Good luck with your investigation."

"Thanks. I have a feeling we're going to need all the luck available for this one."

The technician returned a few moments later carrying an evidence bag full of bundled notes.

"Damn. How much roughly?" Sara asked.

The technician shrugged. "Seven, maybe eight grand. Do you want me to count it now before we get back to base?" He directed his question at Lorraine.

"No. We don't have time. Sara, do you want to take a pic on your phone, and we'll do the same?"

Sara fished her phone out and snapped a few photos. They'd recently had a directive from head office to photograph any money found at the scene of a crime before it was placed in the evidence room because certain cases had been highlighted lately where some money had gone missing during transportation. Sara was all right with the new directive—none of the members of her team would ever dream of pocketing the cash placed in their safety. "Done. I'm off. Be in touch soon."

She returned to speak to Olivia who was waiting anxiously by her car. "The pathologist has it all in hand, and the transportation is being arranged now. You're aware that she'll have to carry out postmortems on your parents?"

"I presumed that would be the case in the circumstances." Her eyes misted up again. "I dread the thought of them being cut open..." Her voice trailed off, and she dabbed a tissue to her eyes.

Sara rubbed Olivia's arm. "I'm sorry, it's a necessary evil. Are your family up to being questioned?"

"I mentioned you wanted to see all my brothers—they're open to that. Anything they can do to help, they will do. I've jotted down their names and addresses for you." She opened a small flowered diary she was holding and tore two pages out and passed them to Sara.

"That's really helpful. I'll be in touch with you soon."

"Thank you, Inspector. Please, please get my parents the justice they deserve."

"I assure you, I'll do my very best." Sara smiled and went in search of Carla. Her partner was just exiting a house four doors down from the Flowers' home. "Anything?"

"Not really. My take is that we're wasting time here. Maybe we should arrange for uniform to conduct the house-to-house and take down any statements that are needed."

"You read my mind. I was about to suggest the same. I've got a list of family members we need to interview. Looks like we're in for a tough day."

"Nothing compared to what the family are going to experience," Carla mumbled as they began their journey back to the car.

CHAPTER 2

He paced the floor, waiting for Mick to arrive. He was on tenterhooks for a reason. He owed the man thousands of pounds. What he had achieved from Ted and Maureen had been an utter disappointment to him. The neighbour knocking on the front door had scared him shitless. He'd snuck out the back of the house and waited in the shadows until the old biddy had returned to her own house. With Mick due any second, he was regretting his decision not to go back inside the property and search for the cash he knew was lying there.

His girlfriend came into the room wearing the shortest T-shirt that barely covered her arse. She stretched, and the T-shirt rose up, revealing the delights he sampled daily, when he was up to it. The previous night, her unwanted attention had suffocated him. He'd left the bed without their usual nightly romping session and ended up sleeping on the couch. He hated himself for what he'd done to the Flowers, especially when the job had gone wrong in more ways than one. He needed those funds. He knew when Mick arrived he was going to pay the price for not coming up with the money he promised he'd pay today.

"Baby, are you still mad at me?" Dawn sauntered towards him, pouting like a ten-pound trout.

He held up his hand to prevent her from coming any closer. "Don't. I ain't got time for this. Mick will be here soon. I suggest you get some clothes on. He'll be wanting compensation for me not being able to cough up the dough he's expecting. He might look at what you can provide as payment."

"What? Fuck that! When's he due?"

He glanced at the clock on the wall. "Ten minutes."

Dawn flew out of the room and upstairs to the bedroom. She emerged fully clothed without visiting the bathroom five minutes later. "How long will he be here?"

"Not sure. Depends on the beating he and his guys are going to want to give me. I'd stay away for the next hour or so. We need some milk. You could always do some shopping."

"Bugger off, I ain't your mother. Do your own shopping."

He stepped forward, ready to slap her.

She retreated a few steps. "Sorry."

"You know what you can do if you don't like what goes on here. Pick up a couple of pints of milk while you're out. You're keen to drink my tea and coffee when you're here, so you can put your frigging hand in your pocket now and again, it won't damn well hurt you."

She scowled at him. "All right. Keep your fucking hair on. I might not come back at all if you keep speaking to me like that."

He gave a nonchalant shrug. "Like you've got an option on that front. Anyway, it suits me either way. Now get out of my face."

She huffed and slammed the front door behind her. He moved over to the window and watched her stomp up the street in her four-inch heels and faux fur jacket and wondered what the hell he saw in her. *Sex, that's what. She's a good lay.*

A car drew up outside the house, and he swallowed the saliva that had instantly filled his mouth. "Shit! He's here." He spun around the room, imitating a headless chicken. Out of the corner of his eye he saw Mick and two of his muscle-bound men walk past the window and up the path.

27

His legs shook. He opened the front door after they rang the bell. Mick brushed him aside and walked into the lounge. The two heavies motioned for him to follow Mick and then they closed the front door and joined them in the lounge.

"Hi, Mick. How's it going?" he asked nervously.

"Cut the crap, dipshit. I'm here for my money. Ten grand."

He swept a hand through his short black hair. "Ah, the truth is, I don't have it yet."

Mick narrowed his eyes and took a step towards him. "Not the right answer, shithead."

He extracted the wallet from his back pocket and handed Mick the five hundred pounds he'd stolen from Ted Flowers. "Take it. It's all I've got."

Mick stared at the money he was holding up. "You're pulling my plonker, right?"

"No. I'm really sorry, Mick. I thought I'd have the cash for you, but a family member let me down at the last minute, man. Take it. It's the best I can do for now."

"Not good enough. I warned you what would happen if you didn't come up with the goods today."

He backed up a few paces. "I'm sorry. I couldn't help it. I promise I'll get you what I owe you by Friday."

"You told me that last week. You broke that promise. Now my boys are going to break you—into tiny pieces."

The two thugs changed positions and stood either side of him, while Mick glared at him.

"Please. Give me one more chance. Up the price, double the amount I owe you if you need to. But, please, don't hurt me. I'm begging you. If you put me in hospital, then I don't have a hope in hell of getting the money for you. Come on, man. You know I'm good for it. I've never let you down in the past, have I?"

Mick contemplated his plea for a moment or two then glanced at one of the bruisers. "Knock him around a bit. He needs to learn a lesson. No broken bones. You can do that later this week if he fails to come up with the money."

"Yes, boss."

For the next few minutes he was pummelled near to death by the thugs, or so it seemed. A couple of punches to each eye forced them to close. He grunted and groaned as the blows rained down on him. "Please…stop. I can't take much more."

The goons ceased their assault when Mick clicked his fingers. He opened his swollen eyes a little to see Mick's feet inches from his head. He sucked in a breath, expecting the man's shoe to connect with his face, and blew out a relieved breath when Mick retreated and made his way to the door.

"You've got until eleven a.m. on Friday to come up with twenty grand. I liked that suggestion of yours. I think it just saved your life. Don't let me down again. Next time I'll tell my boys to finish off the job. Got that?"

The heavies walked away from him.

He struggled to sit upright—his stomach had taken a pounding during the assault. "I've got it. Sorry I let you down. It won't happen again, I promise."

"It better not. Make sure that bitch of yours is here next time."

"Yep, I will. Thanks, Mick. It's always a pleasure doing business with you." He meant the comment sarcastically but ensured it didn't come across that way to either Mick or his cronies. Not that they had two brain cells between them they could rub together.

Hearing the door slam behind them he blew out a relieved breath. Shit! What the fuck was he supposed to do now? How the heck was he supposed to summon up twenty grand in the next few days? He shrugged. It could have been worse. Mick could have demanded he come up with the cash within twenty-four hours, which wasn't an uncommon ploy for him.

Using the chair at the small table to help him rise to his feet, he crossed the room and gingerly walked upstairs to the bathroom. He was tempted not to look at the damage the heavies had caused to his handsome face in the mirror, but there was no getting away from it, the bathroom was tight, and the mirror above the sink was larger than average for the size of the room.

"Shit!" He ran a hand gently over his bruised face. Prodding softly at his cheek bones, he inspected them for any fractures. The bones failed to give way under his fingers. He let out a relieved sigh.

He bathed his face in cold water and then jumped in the shower. While he undressed, he flinched and sucked in sharp breaths from the pain. The bruises were already appearing at regular intervals across his skin. Studying them, he relived the nightmare of the battering he'd endured. The feel of the water on his skin added to his punishment. He only managed to remain under the shower for a few minutes. He stepped out and blotted his skin dry rather than employing the vigorous action he generally used to dry himself.

Staring down at his hands, the only part of him that the thugs hadn't laid into, he knew exactly what would happen when Dawn returned from her trip to the shops. If he was hurting, then so would she.

As if on cue, the front door slammed, and the sound of the kettle being switched on reached him. He finished dressing, opened the window to let the steam out and then left the bathroom. Dawn was preparing the cups with milk and coffee and had her back to him. She must have heard him enter the room because she turned to face him.

She let out a gasp and reached out a hand to touch his face. "Baby, what did the nasty men do to you?"

"Stupid fucking question, bitch."

Before she had the chance to back away, he pounced on her and pounded her to a pulp, matching every blow he'd sustained from the thugs. She screamed and begged for mercy. His anger clouded his judgement, and her face metamorphosed into that of Mick and his goons. His punches increased in intensity.

"You make me sick. You're such a whore. Spread your legs at the drop of a hat."

"No, please, don't do this. What have I done to deserve this? Let me go. I promise I won't go to the police."

"No way. You're going to pay. I've put up with your whining for months." He smashed her in the head a few times until her whining stopped.

Realising he'd taken things too far, he bent down to take a closer look. She wasn't breathing. He should have cared. Should have regretted his actions. Instead, he was furious that she had died on him. He continued to pummel her face with his fists. Momentarily, his own injuries paled into insignificance. Finally, exhausted by his actions, he slumped against the kitchen cabinet and stared at her lifeless body.

He averted his eyes moments later and bowed his head. *How the hell did I do that? Why did I do it? What am I going to do with the body now?*

His exhaustion overwhelmed him—that and the sudden resurgence of his own pain linked together and forced his body to shut down.

He slept for a few hours and woke feeling stiff. He rubbed the back of his neck as he stared at the girl beside him, not one ounce of regret seeping from him. Thoughts of how and where to dump her riffled through his brain. He would need to wait until nightfall before he disposed of her body. An idea struck. He gingerly rose to his feet and left the room. He went upstairs to the bedroom and emerged with an item that would ultimately help dispose of her body.

CHAPTER 3

All the members of the Flowers family lived close to their parents, within a radius of ten miles. Sara called ahead and made arrangements to visit each of the brothers and their families in turn. The first house they called at belonged to the eldest son, David Flowers.

David was looking out the front window when they arrived. Sara and Carla held up their IDs for him to study before he allowed them to enter the house. He lived in a stone-built cottage in the next village to Bodenham, at Bowley. His demeanour was standoffish at first.

"Do you have any idea who would do this to my parents?" he asked, flopping onto a large leather sofa, once he'd shown them through to the lounge. He gestured for Carla and Sara to sit in the easy chairs opposite while his wife left the room to make them all a drink.

"At this early stage, I'm afraid we don't. We're here to ask you and your wife if your parents have been under any kind of stress lately."

"Stress? I'm not sure I follow you."

"Had they fallen out with anyone recently perhaps?"

He shook his head and turned his mouth down as he contemplated the question. "I don't believe so. You think someone they knew did this?"

"That's the route we're taking at this point. Either your father or your mother opened the door and invited the person inside."

His brow furrowed. "How do you know that? Couldn't someone have broken in?"

"There were no signs of a forced entry from what the forensics team could determine."

"Couldn't the person have pushed my parents back when they opened the door?"

Sara nodded her agreement. "That's also a possibility. I have to say we're going to keep an open mind on this one."

"I see. Maybe you haven't really thought about that possibility yet," he replied tartly. "I'm sorry. That was uncalled for."

Sara smiled oozing sympathy. "It's okay. There's really no need for you to apologise."

His wife, Jemima, entered the room and placed a tray on the coffee table in front of her husband and then distributed the cups and saucers.

"They reckon someone who knew Mum and Dad did this, Jemima."

His wife gasped and covered her mouth with her free hand. She sat on the sofa beside her husband and dropped the hand covering her mouth into her lap. "How? Why?" She directed her questions at Sara.

"It's what we believe after we examined the scene. I've already asked your husband, and maybe you'll be able to help us. Did either of your in-laws ever voice any concerns about someone they were in contact with bothering them at all?"

She shook her head. "No. Not that I can recall. I really can't get my head around someone they know doing this to them. That's appalling to even consider. You know they were churchgoers, right?"

"Your sister-in-law mentioned that when we spoke to her earlier. Did they attend the local church?"

"Yes, Bodenham church. They often go there to do the flower arranging for a wedding or…a funeral," Jemima faltered on the last word.

"That's right. Dad has even carried out some repairs to the church in the past, too, without payment. That's the type of chap he was.

Which is why we're struggling to deal with their deaths. We never dreamt anything like this would ever happen in their village." David shook his head and sighed heavily.

"We've spoken briefly to a few of the neighbours, and we're going to get down proper statements during the course of the day. One neighbour in particular saw a man approaching the house. He shrugged it off thinking it was a member of your family paying a visit, said that you guys are frequent visitors."

"That's correct. We're a very close family and call on them regularly to see if they need anything. They never do, because they are, sorry *were*, a very independent couple. This is why we're all so upset that this sort of thing could happen. They've never knowingly hurt anyone in their lives and yet now they're…gone. If the house wasn't broken into, then what are you presuming the motive was?"

"We found a large sum of money under your parents' bed. Your sister told me that they didn't trust banks. My take is that maybe someone known by the immediate family knew about this and tried to take the money."

"Why are you suggesting it's someone to do with our 'immediate family', Inspector?"

"It's simply a theory for now. Were your parents in the habit of telling people they'd only just met that they kept their money hidden in a safe place at the house?"

David's chin dipped onto his chest, and his wife reached for his hand to hold. "Sorry, now I understand what you're getting at." He shuddered. "My God, if it's someone we know well, I'm not sure how we're going to get over this. They were such a genuinely kind couple."

"Maybe I'm barking up the wrong tree, that is why we're planning to interview you all. I appreciate the timing isn't the best, but we do need to get on with our investigation, I'm sure you'll agree?"

"I do. Playing devil's advocate here, maybe it could be someone connected to the church perhaps? The thought of someone close to the family doing this is just abhorrent to me."

"Me too. I can't believe it," Jemima said, sniffling.

Sara glanced sideways to see if Carla was taking notes. She was.

"We'll definitely visit the church and have a word with the vicar. In the meantime, is there anyone within your circle of family and friends that you believe we should call on?"

David and Jemima glanced at each other and shook their heads. "I can't think of anyone, love, can you?" David asked.

"Not off the top of my head. Maybe we'll think it over thoroughly after you've gone and get back to you."

Sara took a sip of coffee from her cup then nodded. "I'll leave you my card. Do you have any children?"

"Yes, Wesley is in Majorca with his girlfriend at the moment. We've decided not to contact him about his grandparents. He'll be devastated; he was extremely close to them. We'll tell him the second he pops in to see us when he returns," David replied. "Our daughter, Mary-Ann, is in Nottingham at present, attending a course. She's a beautician. Again, we haven't informed her. We decided it wouldn't be fair to disrupt either of them."

"I can understand that. We'll need to speak to them in the near future. If you can, tell them to contact me as soon as you've explained the situation to them."

"Of course. You don't think we're doing the wrong thing by not contacting them now, do you?" David asked, frowning.

"No. I think you're absolutely doing the right thing. I'm sure they'll understand the reason behind your delay in telling them."

"The news is going to rock both their worlds."

"I'm sure. Can you recall your parents mentioning if they'd befriended a stranger in the past few months?"

The couple glanced at each other again. "No, what about you, love?" David asked his wife.

"Not that I can think of. Sorry."

"That's okay. Maybe something will jog your memory once we leave." Sara drained her coffee, Carla did the same and they both stood.

Clinging on to each other's hands, David and Jemima showed them to the front door.

"We'll visit the rest of your family and then head back to the station to begin the investigation in earnest. I'm sorry for your loss. I want to assure you that my team and I will do everything we can to bring the person responsible for your parents' deaths to justice. Hopefully within the next few weeks. I'll keep you informed anyway."

David and Jemima shook hands with Sara and Carla, and then David closed the door gently behind them. Sara slammed her fist against her thigh and crossed the gravelled drive to the car. "Damn, they seem a really nice family so far. If the parents were as nice as Olivia and David, then why would someone dream of taking their damn lives? It just doesn't make sense to me."

"Me neither. Heartbreaking it is, bloody heartbreaking," Carla replied.

"Let's not dwell on it for now. We'll move on to another son, Michael, I believe. He lives in the next village." Sara looked at the clock on the dashboard. It was almost twelve-fifteen. She knew it was nearing lunchtime because her tummy was threatening to rumble. "After we've called there, we should keep our eyes open for a small shop where we can pick up a sandwich."

"Dinmore Woods is just up the road. Their café is exceptional."

Sara smiled. "I've not been there. Okay, this one is on me."

"You won't regret it. I used to go up there as a kid with my parents. Fabulous area to take a dog for a walk."

"I could always buy a lead for Misty, I suppose." Sara laughed at the thought of dragging her independent cat around a woodland walk.

"You may laugh. I saw a chap taking his iguana for a walk last year. Nowt so queer as folks as my mum usually likes to say."

"Get out of here. Gosh, the thought of stumbling across one of those in the street puts my bloody teeth on edge."

"Some people adore them. No idea why. I used to have a dog growing up. Alfie. He was a Jack Russell. Crazy as shit, he was. I'd love another one, just not practical with both of us working full time."

"I hate the thought of a dog being left alone in the house for eight hours a day. My friend had a beautiful rough collie, and she used to curse it when she went home to a puddle. It wasn't until I asked her how long she'd left the poor dog alone for, that she realised the damage she was causing to it."

"How long?"

"Over ten hours. Can you imagine being left that long and holding your bladder? In the end she gave it up for adoption. The vet examined it, and she had cystitis, poor pup."

"That's awful. Poor dog. I hope she has a happy home now."

Sara shrugged. "No idea. I barely speak to my friend after treating the dog like that. People simply don't think. Too selfish and wrapped up with their own lives. Okay, that's my whinge for the day."

Carla chuckled. "An acceptable whinge. What's your gut saying about the case, boss?"

"To be honest with you, very little at this stage. I think I'm still going to go along the lines that either a family member did this or someone very close to the family. I could be way off the mark, however. Only time will tell on that one."

Sara fell silent to navigate the narrow country lanes between the two villages. She let out the breath she'd been holding when she drew up outside Michael Flowers' small semi-detached house. It was a stark contrast to David and Jemima's home. "Let's see what we can find out from him."

After ringing the bell, they waited for a good few minutes before the door was finally answered. The man studied them through narrowed eyes. His grey hair was messed up, and the more Sara stared at the man, the more she realised how drunk he was.

"Are you the police?" he slurred.

Sara nodded. "We are, sir. Would it be possible for us to come in and have a quick chat?"

"Can't you do that here? I'm busy, and the place is a mess."

"We'd rather do it inside, if it's all the same to you, sir."

He threw the door back hard—so hard, that when Sara stepped into the house she noted the handle had made a large hole in the wall. She rolled her eyes at her partner and rushed up the passageway and into the lounge to find Michael Flowers stretched out on the sofa, one leg on the floor and the other on the couch. There was a three-quarter-empty bottle of whisky by his side and a glass half-filled with the amber liquid on the side table close to his head.

He was right, the room was a mess. Newspapers were strewn across the floor, and a few dirty dishes were scattered on the coffee table in front of the man. He was staring at the TV, watching a noisy episode of *Loose Women*.

"Can I switch the TV off, Michael?"

"Suit yourself. I'm not watching that shit anyway."

Sara spotted the remote on the sofa behind him. She went to pick it up, and he flinched, which she thought was strange. She pressed the off switch, and the room fell silent.

Sara decided she and Carla should remain standing to question the man. "We're sorry for your loss, sir. Were you close to your parents?"

"What type of question is that?" he mumbled.

"A genuine one."

He struggled to right himself in the chair and picked up his glass. He gulped down a large amount, then said, "Yes. I was very close to them. I'm going to miss the old buggers. They're the only ones who really understood me."

"Are you married, Michael?"

"I used to be until the bitch divorced me."

Sara stared at him. "Have you always had a drink problem?"

He glared at her, anger forcing his eyes wide open. "No. That's not why she left me."

"Did you start drinking after your wife left you, sir?" Sara asked.

"Yes. I did nothing wrong. I'm ill. That's why I had to take early retirement. I've just been diagnosed with Parkinson's Disease."

"I'm sorry to hear that, sir. Do you think drinking yourself into such a state is going to help?"

"I don't know and I don't care. What do I have to live for anyway? My parents are dead, and my wife has left me."

"Do you have any children, sir?"

"Yes, my daughter Paula drops by occasionally. She has her own family to attend to. The last thing she wants to do is tend to her old man after working at the care home all day."

"Which care home, sir?"

"The one in Withington. No idea what the name of it is."

Carla jotted down the information he supplied. "Are you up to answering some questions about your parents, Michael?"

"Depends what you want to know. Their death has hit me hard, harder than I imagined it would. Do you know who did it? Who killed them? If you do, I'd like ten minutes alone with the bastard. Why? Why kill them? Was it a burglary? My parents don't have much."

He bombarded them with questions, and Sara wondered if he would be up for answering any questions she wanted to put to him or whether he was too self-absorbed, turning his own questions over and over in his mind.

"We don't believe it was a burglary, sir. There was no evidence at the scene to make us think that. We don't know who carried out the crime yet, but we intend to find out. We're questioning your relatives in the hope that someone might be able to give us a name."

"What name?"

"Someone you believe might have made contact with your parents in the last few months, perhaps with the sole intention of deliberately befriending them."

"Befriending them? My head's muzzy. Are you saying you think someone gained my parents' trust then killed them?"

"It's all up in the air at present, sir. Maybe that's what happened. Another reason why we're questioning your relatives. Can you recall anyone who could likely fit the bill?"

He took another swig of whisky, rolled it around his mouth and then swallowed. "I don't know is the honest answer. Our family is really tight. We don't tend to let in many outsiders, at least I don't think we do. I'm not sure now." He ran a hand across his stubble as if confused.

Sara sighed. She had a feeling they weren't going to obtain anything useful from this man, either because of his illness or more likely because of the alcohol he had consumed. "Can we ring anyone to come and be with you, sir, at this sad time?"

"No. I need to wallow in self-pity for the people I have lost over the past few years. I'm sorry I can't supply you with the information you need. Please, please do your best to find this person. Mum and Dad didn't deserve to go out of this stinking world like that."

"We will. I'm concerned about you, Michael. Are you sure you're going to be okay when we leave?"

"I'm sure. I'm used to being by myself. Mum and Dad used to drop by periodically, and although my brothers and I are close, I don't like to bother them with my tales of woe."

"Okay. You take care. I'll leave you one of my cards if you should think of anything, umm…when you're thinking straight."

He tried to stand but flopped back in his chair. "You mean when I'm sober?"

Sara smiled. "Take care."

"Thank you. Do your best. Any idea when we'll be able to put them to rest?" He flapped a hand in front of him. "Tell one of my other brothers, they'll pass the message on when the time is right. Not sure I can take it all in now."

"We'll do that. Stay there, we'll see ourselves out." Sara left a card on the table close to him. Again, he flinched as she got close.

Sara and Carla left the house. "Bloody hell, it's barely twelve-forty-five and he's already pissed," Carla said over the roof of the car.

"Let's not dwell on that for now. We haven't got a clue how much of his drinking is down to the loss of his parents. I'd feel bad judging him on this visit."

"Maybe it's guilt. Perhaps he killed his parents and is finding it impossible to live with the consequences."

Sara raised her eyes to the sky when a large drop of rain landed on her nose. "Get in before we get soaked." Once they were in the car, she replied to Carla's suggestion. "I think you're wrong, by the way. I don't think he'd have it in him to kill them."

Carla shrugged. "You're probably right."

"Now, where's this café you spoke about? I'm in dire need of suste-nance. You'll have to give me directions."

"No worries. It's only ten minutes from here. They do fabulous cream teas as well, if you fancy one?"

Sara smiled and slotted the car into gear. She flipped the switch, and the wiper blades cleared the windscreen as the heavens opened. "We might get a little wet at the other end."

"It'll be worth it, I promise."

They parked in the car park. Carla shot out of the car to buy the parking ticket. She returned and stuck the ticket on the inside of the windscreen and then bolted back to the café. Sara placed her jacket over her head and raced across the car park to join her. "Bloody hell. I know July has been arid and we're in desperate need of rain, but this is ridiculous."

There was a small queue ahead of them. They both chose a cheese and ham panini and a small latte. "We better have one of your delicious scones and cream, too," Sara told the young woman behind the counter.

"Do you want a scone between you? They're quite big."

"I think we'd better, thanks." Sara paid for lunch and carried the coffees over to one of the benched tables at the rear.

"Thanks for this, boss. My treat next time. Where are we going after lunch?"

"You're welcome." She flipped open her notebook and ran her finger down the list of names. "Stuart Flowers. His address is in Risbury. I have to admit, I haven't heard of that village. Do you know where it is?"

"Not far up the road. About five or ten minutes, I suppose. We're not having much luck so far, are we?"

"It's early days yet. Their minds are with their parents. Once they've had the chance to grieve properly, I'm sure we'll get a few calls. At least I hope that's the case."

The waitress arrived with their paninis.

Sara smiled at the woman and pushed her cup and saucer to one side. "Wow! That was quick."

"We aim to please. Do you want me to bring your scone out now or in a few minutes?"

"Whichever suits you. Thanks, this looks delicious."

The waitress nodded and rushed back through the swing door, emerging a few seconds later with two plates, a fruit scone, jam and a pot of clotted cream. Sara felt her waistband tighten at the feast in front of her. "Thanks." When the waitress left the table, Sara blew out a breath and leaned forward to say, "Blooming heck, I think I've gained ten pounds just looking at this lot. I'm never going to manage to eat it all, no matter how scrumptious it all is."

"Get on with you. Think of it as your main meal. You could always have a tin of soup for tea when you get home tonight."

Sara puffed out her cheeks at the thought of having to eat yet another meal that day—she didn't have the healthiest of appetites as it was. "Is that the voice of experience talking? How do you manage to eat so much and stay so slim?"

"I have a healthy sex life, what more can I say?"

Sara had taken a mouthful of her panini and almost spat it out. She glanced around at the other tables to see if any of the other diners had heard what Carla had announced loudly. "Bloody hell! Do you want to tell the whole world that?"

Carla burst into laughter. "Wow! I would never have taken you for being a prude."

Sara's mouth gaped open for a moment before she replied, "I am not! I just don't think it's appropriate to shout about something like that during the course of lunch in a packed café when there are children present."

Carla searched around her and then shook her head. "I hardly class an eighteen-month-old child focussing on its food corruptible. Like I said, you're a prude."

Sara didn't have the heart to challenge her partner any further. Instead, she took another nibble out of her panini.

"Umm...while we're on the subject of sex, if you don't think it's too personal a question, do you have a boyfriend or husband?" Carla asked.

Sara kept her gaze on her plate. She knew her partner would utter those words one day. She counted herself lucky that she appeared to have got away with it for eighteen months. She remained silent, considering how she should answer. Her reluctance to reveal the truth weighed heavily on her shoulders. "Can we talk about that another time? I don't feel as though this is the right time to share my personal life with you just yet."

Carla seemed offended, hurt even.

Sara instantly regretted uttering the words. "Sorry, Carla. I didn't mean to upset you. I'll tell you when I'm ready, I promise. At the moment, it's still too hard for me to deal with."

"I apologise for putting you on the spot. I misread the signs that we were finally getting on with each other, dare I say becoming friends even. Sorry to have misconstrued that notion."

Sara's heart sank. She pushed her half-eaten panini away from her and took a sip of coffee. "I'm sorry, I didn't mean that to sound so harsh. I'm a private person. Please don't take that personally. What I will tell you is that up to this point in my thirty-two years on this earth, I've known great sadness that most individuals would find abhorrent."

"No, it's me who should be apologising, not you. Forget I said anything. I will say one thing, though…"

Sara tilted her head and asked, "What's that?"

"Feel free to share in the future. I'm a damn good listener and I like you, DI Sara Ramsey. Your distance at work sometimes is very notice-able. Anyway, if I can share about my sex life with you in a café, feel free to share what dark secrets lie in your past whenever you feel the need."

Sara chuckled. "I promise I will one day. Feel free to keep your own sex life and what it entails private in the future."

"Deal." Carla sniggered and bit a large chunk of her panini then pushed the rest of it away from her and pulled the plate with the scone and cream towards her. "Want me to divide it up?"

"If you insist. A smaller half for me, if you don't mind." Sara was relieved to see that Carla wasn't the type to hold a grudge, but she felt a little hurt that her colleague found her distant. Was it just Carla who felt that way or did the rest of her team think the same? Either way, she had no intention of breaking down in front of them and spilling the heartache she had suffered in recent years.

Carla was right about one thing. The cream tea was to die for and totally worth the extra inch or so on her waistband.

CHAPTER 4

They left the café half an hour later. The strained atmosphere
that had descended upon them now appeared to be in the
past. Once they were seated in the car, Sara looked up the
address for the next brother they were due to see and swivelled in her
seat. "I will tell you one day. All I ask is that you don't hold it
against me."

Carla nodded. "It's a deal with an added proviso."

"Which is?"

"That if you need to unburden yourself at any time, you have my
permission to bend my ear or dampen my shoulder with your tears."

Sara held out her hand. Carla shook it. "That's a deal." Selecting
first gear, she crawled out of the car park, noting the five-mile-an-hour
speed limit. "Let's get the rest of the interviews out of the way and
head back to base."

They arrived at Stuart Flowers' detached home ten minutes later.
There was a silver BMW sitting in the drive. A smart woman in her
fifties opened the door.

"Hello, Mrs Flowers. I'm DI Sara Ramsey, and this is my partner,
DS Carla Jameson."

"Yes, we've been expecting you. You're very welcome to come in; however, Stuart just rang to say he's going to be a little late. Some emergency happened at the restaurant this morning that he needs to deal with. Can I get you a coffee while you wait?"

"No, thank you, Mrs Flowers, we've just had lunch. Is your husband going to be long? We have another one of his brothers to see. Maybe we should slot him in first and come back later."

"Whatever suits you. I'm sure my husband won't be more than ten minutes or so. Maybe I can fill in some details for you in his absence."

"That's fine with us."

"Come through to the lounge."

They followed her through the large hallway into a spacious lounge that would have been well at home sitting on the pages of a glossy interior magazine.

"You have a beautiful home, Mrs Flowers. Have you lived here long?"

"Gosh, I suppose the past twenty years or so. We've recently updated all the rooms. My mother-in-law, rest her soul, helped me pick out the fabrics for the curtains throughout. She had a wonderful eye for colours. I shall miss her terribly."

"Mind if we take a seat?" Sara asked tentatively.

"I'm sorry. Of course."

The three of them sank into the super comfy sofas.

"Perhaps you can tell us when you last saw your in-laws?"

Mrs Flowers thought the question over for a second or two and then bashed her fist against her temple. "I had lunch with them last Wednesday, although Stuart dropped by to see them both on Friday of last week. He always takes them a joint of meat or two to put in their freezer when he gets a delivery."

"That's nice of him. I'm sure they appreciated that."

Mrs Flowers nodded, and her eyes misted up with tears. "All the family tried to do their bit to help out. The cost of living is so high nowadays. Not that Mum and Dad ever struggled to pay the bills, but it doesn't hurt to give back to your relatives now and again, does it?"

"Quite right. Just by interviewing the rest of the family members we've gleaned how much they were loved by you all."

"They were. What do you know about what happened to them, can you tell me?"

Before Sara could answer, the front door slammed, and a rotund man with thinning grey hair rushed into the lounge. "I'm so sorry I'm late. An emergency I had to attend to came up. I know this is an important meeting with a family emergency of our own to attend to, but needs must."

"Hello, Mr Flowers. Don't worry, we haven't been here long ourselves. I'm DI Sara Ramsey, the SIO in your parents' case, and this is my partner, DS Carla Jameson."

He shook his head and raked a trembling hand through his hair. "Terrible blow to hear the news this morning. I thought Olivia was joking when she rang me. It was such a surreal conversation. The only way I can describe it is that I felt I was having an out-of-body experience. The moment she mentioned our parents had been murdered..." He paused to take a deep breath then continued, "I've been in shock ever since. Yes, I had an emergency to deal with at work, which briefly took my mind off the horrendous news, but driving home I was on autopilot. Don't even remember getting in my car, let alone navigating the damn thing home."

Sara was used to people talking fast in instances such as this and smiled at the man as he chuntered on. "That's understandable. Before we give the investigation our full attention, I wanted to speak to the family first. We've visited two of your brothers so far and asked them if your parents had befriended anyone who had caused you to have any doubts at all."

"What have my brothers said? Because for the life of me I can't think of anyone that fits the bill. My parents were loved by everyone in the surrounding villages, not just their own. They've never knowingly had a cross word with anyone. You know they attended church regularly, don't you?"

"So we've been told. Honestly, we've heard nothing but good

things about your parents from other family members, plus, more importantly, their neighbours also. At present, we're unsure how or why they were targeted. Obviously, the more you can share with us, the more likely we are to solve the case quickly. I know the timing could be better, what with your emotions registering so high…"

"I completely get where you're coming from, Inspector. My family and I will do everything we can to answer your questions, no matter how probing we think they are. All we want is for you to find the person who has robbed us of two wonderful people."

"Thank you. We're going to need your support on this one. Do you have any children?"

Stuart walked over and sat next to his wife. He clasped her tiny hand in his large one. "No. Sadly, we lost a child a few weeks after it was born. Our daughter had a heart defect. We made the heartbreaking decision not to try for another child. Couldn't bring ourselves to go through the same thing again."

"I'm sorry to hear that. I don't know how to put this without it sounding insensitive—have you ever had a reason to doubt any member of your family? Either your siblings or their children?"

Stuart shook his head and glanced at his wife. "Sylvia? Have you?"

"No, never. We all get on well. We appreciate that Michael has had a rough time of it lately, but we've all tried to support him as much as we can without it impacting our own lives."

Sara smiled. "He does appear to be very troubled. Not wishing to speak out of turn, but you might want to drop by and see him later."

"Don't tell me he was hitting the bottle?" Stuart asked.

"Yes, unfortunately. I think your parents' death has hit him hard."

"It's hit us all hard. We have to deal with it, though. Drowning his bloody sorrows in alcohol isn't going to bring them back," Stuart replied.

Sylvia turned to look at her husband. "That's a bit harsh, love. He's been through hell the last year. He's not as strong as you, you know that."

"I know, love. But he also needs to remember that he's ill and should be taking far better care of himself than he's doing at present.

48

I'll ring Paula later, she'll get him back on the right track in no time at all."

Sylvia nodded her agreement.

"That would be wonderful," Sara said. "Okay, if there's nothing more you can tell us, we'll leave now. Here's my card should you either need to call me or if you think of anything I should know." She stood and crossed the room to hand the card to Stuart.

"Thank you. I'll show you out."

He walked them to the front door, his shoulders slumped. "Please, do your best for us."

"I promise we will. Sorry to drag you away from your work."

"No problem. I had every intention of coming home early to be with Sylvia anyway. I know how much my parents meant to her. Treasure your parents while you've still got them, Inspector, because you never know what lies around the next corner."

"I will. My condolences once again. I'll be in touch soon."

He nodded and closed the door behind them.

Sudden tears sprang to Sara's eyes while she made her way to the car. Luckily, she wasn't the type to wear mascara, or any other type of heavy makeup come to that, so there was no chance of it getting spoilt. She opened the car door and sneakily swiped her eyes on the sleeve of her jacket as she slipped into her seat.

"Are you all right?" Carla asked, a concerned expression wrinkling her brow.

"There was me thinking I'd got away with it. I'm fine. It's just that now and then things sneak up on me."

Carla shrugged and patted her shoulder. "My offer still stands."

Sara waved a hand in front of her. "I'll be fine, don't worry about me. Right, one last brother to interview."

"I hope he's more forthcoming with a name. I think this case is going to be stuck in the middle of nowhere if he can't."

"I was thinking along the same lines. So frustrating. Maybe the person stopped by the house on the off-chance after all."

"I'm on the fence with that notion."

"Yep, me too. Forget I ever mentioned it." Sara turned the key in the ignition and pulled away from the house.

Allan Flowers was the only brother left to see on their list. Sara said a silent prayer, hoping he would be able to fill in the large blank standing in their path.

CHAPTER 5

Allan Flowers lived in another exceptionally well-presented detached home in the village of Urdimarsh. The house was full of character, and yet Sara suspected it was a new-build on a small estate of six houses on the edge of the quaint village.

"Another village I didn't know existed. I really need to get out more." Sara yanked on the handbrake and switched off the engine.

"There are hundreds of villages like this in the area, and yes, you need to get out to explore the beautiful county you now call your home."

Sara giggled. "Thanks for chastising me. I'll put it on my extensive to-do list."

"Sorry. I didn't mean to preach. It's just that so many live in this area, and all I hear them complain about is that there's nothing to do. All right, it might not be an area full of tourist attractions such as London, but bloody hell, look around you at the fabulous landscape."

"I agree. It gets to me that it has taken a gruesome murder investigation for me to realise what a wonderful county this is."

They exited the vehicle and walked across the deep gravelled drive to the large oak door and rang the ornate bell attached to the stone façade.

A young blonde woman wearing a velour jogging suit opened the door. Her eyes were red and swollen.

"Hello there. I'm DI Sara Ramsey, and this is DS Carla Jameson. We've come to see Allan Flowers."

"Come in. I'm Samantha. Dad is in the garden out back."

Sara entered the house and asked, "Thanks, Samantha. How has your father taken the news?"

"Badly. Even though it was raining heavily, he insisted on tending the plants in the garden. That's his means of escape out there. I tried to call him, but he was having none of it. Hopefully, you coming to see him will force him inside. Do me a favour and refuse to go out to him."

Sara smiled. "Of course. We got drenched just before lunch. If he's been out there all this time he'll make himself ill."

"He didn't even bother to put a coat on either. I suppose I better stock up on cold remedies just in case he comes down with the lurgies."

"He's aware that we're coming."

"I'll give him a shout and then make some coffee, if you'd like one?"

"Thanks, we're fine."

They followed Samantha through the house into an open-plan living area that was simply breathtaking. Samantha invited them to take a seat in the lounge area while she dipped out into the garden to fetch her father.

Carla nudged Sara. "Blimey. I thought the last house was gorgeous, but this place takes the bloody biscuit. Do you think there's a bit of one-upmanship going on between the siblings?"

Sara shrugged. "Who knows? This place must have cost a pretty penny or two to build. Makes my new-build feel like an inadequate doll's house in comparison. Something to aspire to, right?"

"Aspire to? Maybe if I won the lottery. I'd never be able to afford a place this beautiful otherwise. I'm definitely envious. I've never been inside a house as stunning as this one."

Carla and Sara both jumped when a male voice behind them said,

"Thank you. I had a vision, and an architect friend of mine came up with this design."

"You're extremely lucky to have found someone able to create what you envisaged, sir. I'm DI Sara Ramsey, and this is my partner, DS Jameson. Would you like to take a moment to dry yourself off? We're not in a rush."

"Thank you. I'll nip and get a quick change of clothes. Won't keep you more than five minutes."

He left the room. Sara and Carla turned around, taking in all the sumptuous details of their surroundings. Samantha appeared at the edge of the kitchen area. "Are you sure I can't tempt you to have a coffee from our super-duper machine? It's no bother."

"Go on then, you've twisted my arm. Carla?"

"I'd love one, too. Can I watch?"

Samantha laughed. "Of course you can, there's really nothing to it."

Ever inquisitive, both Sara and Carla crossed the room and stood by the kitchen island while Samantha expertly measured out the coffee and placed it in the contraption which she then inserted into the machine. Then she filled a section of the machine with water. The three of them watched the coffee pour into a clear jug. The whole process took barely three minutes to complete. Samantha poured the coffee, added cream and sugar and handed them both a small cup and saucer.

Sara smelt the richness of the coffee beans and then took a sip. "Wow! I've tasted some really great coffee in my time, but this is absolutely exceptional. I might invest in one of those machines for the office. What do you think, Carla?"

"I'd go halves with you if it was only you and me to enjoy it. I think the boys would ruin it within a week, though."

Sara cringed. "Maybe you have something there. I might see about getting one for home instead. A necessary luxury for all coffee drinkers, I believe."

"We love it. Dad reckons it's the best investment he's ever made in the house. So glad you're enjoying it." She leaned over the counter top to add, "They're really not that expensive either. A couple of hundred pounds, I think."

Just then, Allan Flowers entered the room, his hair still damp and combed into place. He'd changed his wet clothes for a virtually replica ensemble of dark jeans and a brown jumper. "I'm glad my daughter is looking after you so well. What do you think of the coffee?"

"She is. It's superb. I've just said how much I'd like a machine myself. I have a new-build. Unfortunately, it didn't come with any added extras such as this."

They all laughed. Sara felt relieved to have pulled the man out of his grief if only for a short time.

"Bring your cups, we'll make ourselves comfortable in the lounge area. I'm sorry for the delay. Mum and Dad's death knocked the stuffing out of me this morning. The only way I know of coping with that kind of upset is to tend to my garden."

Sara glanced over her shoulder. "You've done it justice. It looks stunning, just like your beautiful home."

"Thank you. I really wasn't fishing for compliments."

"I know. Credit where it's due, though. First of all, I'd like to say how very sorry I am to meet you under such circumstances."

"It's Olivia I feel sorry for, having to witness Mum and Dad in that state. We all wanted to go over there to be with her, but she begged us not to. She said it would be much better remembering them the way they used to be rather than how she found them. She'll have to live with that image for the rest of her life."

"It is very sad when a relative discovers the body of a deceased family member. We can offer her some counselling if that's what she needs to get over this."

"I'll make sure she's aware of that. Thank you, Inspector. Now, how can we help?"

"I've asked the same question of your brothers—we'd like to know if either of your parents mentioned if they had befriended anyone lately or if they'd possibly fallen out with someone that you know about."

His chest inflated when he inhaled a large breath. "I truly can't think of anyone. However, although we were exceptionally close as a family, I wouldn't necessarily say that we were in each other's pockets. They were active members of the local church. Maybe they met someone there that they didn't think to mention. What did my brothers say?"

"Very similar to yourself, to be honest with you. We'll be sure to drop by and pay the vicar a visit, see if he can shed any light on things for us."

"I think that would be the best bet. I'm sorry we can't help you further. My parents were very likeable characters."

"So we've been led to believe." Sara took another refreshing sip of her coffee and placed her empty cup on the table. She glanced at Carla, who was also in the process of draining her cup, just as another young woman walked into the room.

"Dad?"

"I'm here, Daphne." Allan leapt out of his chair and gathered the woman in his arms, smoothing her brunette hair down her back.

She pulled out of her father's arms. "Why? How could this happen? Have the police said anything?"

Allan pointed at Sara and Carla who were walking towards the pair of them. "The police are here now."

"Here? What are you doing here? You should be out there scouring the streets, looking for the person who did this, not here drinking our coffee. How dare you!"

"Now, Daphne. Calm down. They have to begin their investigation somewhere," Allan reprimanded his daughter.

Daphne's anger didn't visibly lessen when she glared at Sara and Carla.

Sara smiled weakly at her. "We're sorry for your loss. We understand how hard—"

"No, you don't. You haven't got the foggiest idea how much Granddad and Grandma were loved, adored by this family."

"Daphne, be fair," Samantha pleaded, joining her father and sister.

Sara raised her hand in front of her. "I understand you being upset, but we still need to make enquiries with loved ones before we can start our investigation. I'm sorry if you think we're going about our work the wrong way." Her tone was one of disappointment. She hadn't often come up against an objectionable family member in the past in such circumstances, but when she had, the put-down usually made them rethink their rudeness.

Daphne dropped her head in shame and flopped into the chair beside her. She buried her head in her hands and sobbed. Samantha and their father both comforted her.

"I apologise for my behaviour…Nan and Granddad meant the absolute world to us. I just can't believe we won't ever see them again," Daphne finally said.

"There's really no need for you to apologise. We're used to dealing with people who are grieving. Grief affects us all very differently. Samantha and Daphne, can I ask if you know of anyone who your grandparents have accepted into their lives recently?"

Both girls shook their heads before Daphne said, "No. I really can't believe that someone they had welcomed into their home would do this."

Samantha shrugged. "Maybe this has something to do with the church. Could they have met someone in the congregation who wasn't legitimate? Maybe that person pretended to be homeless or something along those lines. I might be grasping at straws, but surely it would be worth a visit."

"You're right. We intend dropping by the church immediately after we've spoken to you."

"Good. I really don't think we can give you anything more helpful than that, Inspector. That disappoints us as much as you," Allan insisted.

"Very well. We'll be off then. I'll leave you a card. Don't hesitate to get in touch with me if you either think of anything or want to ask how the investigation is going, although I will be keeping in contact with your sister regularly. Maybe you should ring her often for an update."

"Olivia will keep us in the loop. Thank you, Inspector. We hope to hear some good news from you soon," Allan replied. He turned and walked back up the hallway to the front door. He shook their hands, holding on to Sara's a little longer than anticipated. "I'm not sure I should be saying this at all, but here goes...I'm willing to put up a reward for any information from the public."

"That's very kind of you. Maybe you should hold fire on that for now. In the next day or two I'll be arranging a media appeal. If we don't glean anything from that, I can always go back to the media and get them to run the story again mentioning the reward you're willing to offer."

He nodded. "Whichever way you want to play things is fine by me. I want the bastard who has destroyed my family caught and thrown behind bars. If that person reveals themselves in our midst within the next few days, I'm liable to throttle them."

Sara sighed. "Please try and restrain yourself, Mr Flowers. If someone pops up on your radar, you'd be advised to ring me before wading in there and getting yourself into trouble for any vigilante intentions you may have."

"I understand what you're saying. Surely you can recognise what an effort that would be on my part—not to strike out, I mean."

"I reiterate, it would be foolish of you to vent your anger on the person and not contact me first. Why take the risk of ending up in prison yourself?"

"It would make me feel a darn sight happier knowing that I whipped the fucker's arse who murdered my parents."

Sara nodded. "Just ring me if a name surfaces, please?"

Reluctantly he agreed.

They stepped out of the house and made their way back to the car.

"I can understand where he's coming from," Carla noted, dropping into the passenger seat beside Sara.

"Yep. I'd be very tempted to do the same if ever my parents lost their lives in such a dreadful manner."

"What now?"

"I was going to shoot back to the station, but I think we should pay the vicar at their local church a visit instead."

"I'm with you on that one. Might as well get all the interviews out of the way in one day."

"Agreed. I feel badly for this family. It's obvious how much they all thought of their parents. Let's dig deep on this case to find a swift resolution."

"We always give our all to a case, boss."

"I know. I'm simply saying that I think we should add more effort to this one. As you rightly said, it's not often we get this type of heinous crime on our patch. The quicker we solve it, the more the public are going to appreciate our efforts."

"Providing nothing stands in our way, let's hope that comes to fruition."

CHAPTER 6

Sara parked the car outside Bodenham church. Together, she and Carla walked inside to find a man of the cloth rearranging the hymn books at the end of one of the aisles. Sara showed the vicar her ID, and after introducing herself and her partner said, "I'm not sure if you're aware of what has happened to Mr and Mrs Flowers, father."

"Unfortunately, I'm fully aware, Inspector. You can't keep those kinds of details quiet for long in a village of this size. It's utterly appalling that this type of crime should be committed in this area—in any area come to that. If I can do anything to assist the investigation, you only have to ask."

"Actually, we wondered if you had noticed a change in the Flowers recently."

He placed his hand to his chin as he thought. "No. I can't say I have. Maureen and Ted were two of the most genuinely friendly people in my congregation. They would do anything for anyone if you asked them to. I can't believe someone could hurt such a wonderful couple. Hurt, I say, I mean kill. I'm quite shocked to be honest. I needed to keep my mind active today, thought I'd come down and potter around here rather than sit at home contemplating what that poor couple went through in the final hours of their lives." His eyes brimmed with tears.

"Do you want to take a seat for a moment?" Sara asked, gripping his arm as his legs gave way a little beneath him.

"Thank you. My health isn't so good at the moment. I've been diagnosed with cancer, you see. It's terminal. My flock have no idea about my illness. I put on a brave face during my sermons."

"My heart goes out to you, father," Sara replied, her chest squeezing a touch.

"Thank you. At least I'm still alive, for now. Unlike Ted and Maureen. Do you have any idea who carried out this deplorable act?"

"At present, no. We're conducting enquiries today and then we'll crack on with the investigation once we've collated any useful information together. I hear they spent a lot of time helping out around here, father."

"They did. A charming couple who always put others first. That's why I can't understand this happening to them. What could be the motive behind someone killing them?"

"We're at a loss about that right now. There was no evidence of a forced entry; however, Mr Flowers' wallet was missing from their home."

"Money? Are you telling me that people resort to killing another person just to take the contents of their wallet?"

Sara nodded. "It looks that way. Although there was a vast sum of money kept at the couple's house that the intruder wasn't aware of— unless he or she was aware and got disturbed during the search of the property. However, we didn't see any signs of the home being ransacked at all."

"How odd. It's unthinkable that two people have lost their lives for the sake of a few pounds. Just unthinkable."

"Is your congregation full of regulars, father?"

"Mostly, yes. Of course, we'll get the odd person calling in here if they're on holiday, visiting the area."

"Have you noticed any strangers here lately?"

He bowed his head to ponder the question. "I honestly can't think of anyone."

"Perhaps a homeless person looking for the odd handout?"

"There's nothing coming to mind. We don't tend to get homeless people around here, Inspector. Maybe in the city, but not out here in the sticks."

"Which is what I suspected. Do you recall the Flowers getting closer than normal to a member of the congregation?"

"Not really. All my parishioners are friendly towards each other. I know not every vicar can say the same about their flock, but I can say that with a large amount of confidence."

"That's definitely reassuring for us to hear. Did they ever confide in you about any relatives perhaps?"

"All the time. May I ask in what context…oh, no, you surely can't mean that you suspect one of their relatives of doing this?"

"It's something that we have to consider, father, although we've spent most of the day speaking with the couple's children, and nothing struck me as odd about any of them."

"I'm glad to hear it. I hate the thought of one of their children being responsible for their deaths."

"In that case, we have no further questions for you, father. May I leave you a card? In the hope that you will ring me if you hear anything on the grapevine, so to speak."

"Of course, I'll call you. Anything I can do to help, you only have to ask."

"One last thing before we go. Could you keep an ear to the ground for us? Maybe you'll overhear something that doesn't sit well with you."

"I don't do confessions here, if that is what you're asking, Inspector. This is a Church of England church."

"I appreciate that, father. That's not what I was implying. If you overhear something in general, that's all."

"You have my word on that. Good luck with your investigation."

Sara inhaled a weary breath. "Thank you. We'll take all the luck thrown in our direction. Don't forget to ring me if you hear anything."

"I won't. Nice to meet you both."

"You too, father. Take care of yourself."

"You're very kind. Thank you."

Sara's and Carla's footsteps echoed around the substantial church as they left.

Carla shuddered when they reached the car. She peered back over her shoulder and whispered, "Sorry, stupid thing for me to say, but those places give me the creeps."

Sara chuckled. "Get in the car."

They arrived back at the station to find the rest of the team hard at work. Carla bought two coffees while Sara jotted down the information they had gathered during the course of the day on the whiteboard, which to date, was disappointingly non-existent for such a major crime.

Carla placed a cup on the desk close to the whiteboard.

"Thanks, I thought I'd be all coffeed out by now but I'm not. My head is buzzing. Not sure if that's the start of a headache brewing or what."

"What do you want me to do?"

"Go round the rest of the team, see if they've managed to locate anything useful that we can work with regarding the family. My guess is they haven't. I'll continue noting down all the names on the board. No, wait, before you do that, can you get in touch with the press office? Ask them to arrange a media conference at their earliest convenience. Push for tomorrow if you can. I'd like to get the word circulating about this ASAP."

Carla rushed back to her desk. "On it now. Any preference for morning or afternoon?"

"Not really. Just ask them for the earliest slot they can arrange. I don't want to delay that side of things if at all possible."

The black marker pen flew across the whiteboard. By the time Carla reported back to her, Sara had written down the names of all the family members they had spoken to that morning. "How did you get on?"

"Eleven tomorrow morning suits you?"

"Sounds fine. Let's hope nothing else crops up in the meantime. Can you do me a favour after you've gone around the room?"

"What's that?"

"Jot down the names of any relatives we didn't manage to speak to. Any of the Flowers' grandkids living in the area. We'll set aside some time to visit them over the next few days."

"Will do." Carla crossed the room and stopped at Craig's desk first.

Sara noted out of the corner of her eye that Carla didn't stay there long before she moved on to Christine's desk.

By the time she had completed her chore, Carla joined her with an update. "Nothing so far, boss. Everyone seems squeaky clean."

Sara shrugged. "Why am I not surprised? The only person I really had any doubt about was Michael. I guess all he's guilty of is taking his parents' deaths harder than his siblings. All right, it's almost knocking-off time. Why don't we leave things there for now and begin afresh in the morning?"

"I think that's a great idea."

"I need to arrange a squad car to do regular check-ups around the Bodenham area before I go home."

CHAPTER 7

W ithin half an hour, Sara was back in her car heading along A49 towards her home in Walkers Green. She had to resist the temptation to stop off and visit her parents, opting to ring her mother after she had seen to Misty and made herself some tea, although she was still stuffed from lunchtime.

Misty wound herself around her legs the second she stepped over the threshold. She swept her adorable cat into her arms and smothered her with kisses. Misty purred her delight at the over-the-top attention she was fond of receiving at the end of Sara's long day. "Hungry, baby?"

Misty struggled out of her arms and raced through the house into the kitchen. Sara laughed, slipped out of her shoes at the front door and followed Misty. She stopped at the larder cupboard close to the kitchen door and removed a can of cat food. Misty almost tripped her up during her journey over to the sink to retrieve the dedicated spoon she kept on the draining board for 'cat food use only'. "Will you be patient, Munchkin?"

After feeding the cat, she filled the kettle and opened the fridge, debating whether she would regret not eating another meal before bedtime. "Nah, if I'm hungry later, I'll have some cheese and biscuits."

She left Misty scoffing her food and walked into the lounge. After placing her coffee on the side table, she sought out her mobile and rang her parents' number. She cringed when she realised it was six-thirty, the time they usually sat down for their evening meal.

Her father answered the phone; he sounded a little irate. "Hello."

"Sorry, Dad, it's only me. I didn't realise what the time was until the phone started ringing. Enjoy your dinner, I'll call back in an hour or so. I'll jump in the bath instead."

"Very well, love. Speak soon."

Sara ended the call and ran up the stairs to her all-white pristine bathroom. Being a new-build, all the walls were painted white throughout the house. She'd had strict instructions not to decorate for a year, giving the house time to breathe during the drying-out process. She had noticed a few fine cracks here and there, nothing too alarming compared to some of the horror stories she'd heard about new-builds in a TV documentary recently. If she'd seen that programme before moving in she would have been put off ever buying a new property in the future. Thankfully, no one else on the estate had mentioned they'd had any issues with any of their homes, a blessed relief to Sara's ears. She didn't have time for that crap. She inspected the house thoroughly every Sunday, noting down if any new cracks had appeared during that week. Nothing too taxing had reared its head so far. She knew that when the time came for decorating, her father would offer his services —he was a dab hand at hanging wallpaper. Sara collected interior design magazines and had even created a mood board for the colour scheme she wanted eventually. But that wouldn't take place for another six months or so yet.

She ran the bath and dipped into the master bedroom to collect a clean pair of pyjamas and her towelling robe. Misty ran up the stairs to join her. She hopped up onto the bed and preened herself while Sara undressed and threw her dirty clothes in the large Ali Baba basket she had treated herself to a few weeks ago.

The bath took only a few minutes to fill. She stepped into the lavender bubbles and sighed. "This is ecstasy. Maybe I should suggest putting a bath in my office at work, especially when I have to work late...or maybe not," she reconsidered, when she remembered most of her team were males.

In the distance, her mobile rang. "Damn! I forgot to bring it upstairs." She strained her neck to hear how long the caller would leave it before they left a voicemail. A beep sounded not long after, letting her know that a message had been left. Who the heck could that be? She debated whether to leave the tub and run downstairs to find out but decided against wetting her new carpets in the end. "I'll pick up the message later. They'll ring back if it's urgent."

Switching off mentally, she reclined her head against the bath and closed her eyes. It took all her strength not to drift off. If she fell asleep now, she knew it would be impossible to sleep later when she eventually went to bed.

After a long soak, she felt refreshed and at ease. Slipping into her pyjamas and towelling robe, she ventured downstairs again and poured herself a vodka and tonic then settled on the couch to ring her parents. It was then that she remembered she'd received a message. She dialled the number and listened.

"Hi, Sara, it's me. Sorry I had to dash off last week. I wondered if it would be possible to see you again—soon. Ring me back. Bye."

Sara's heart rate shot up at the sound of his voice. She flopped back in the couch and took a gulp of her drink. "Crap! What do I do now?" Donald was her husband Philip's brother. The previous week they had met up for a drink with the intention of consoling each other over his death, only it hadn't worked out that way. With their emotions running high, they had ended up kissing. The kiss had lasted for the briefest moment, but since then, every time Sara thought about the incident, a cold shiver ran through her. It was too soon after Philip's death to even contemplate getting involved with another man. There was no way on earth if she did settle down with someone new, that person should or would be Donald. How the hell was she supposed to let him down gently? The second the kiss had ended, she'd thought they'd both realised what a mistake it was. *Guess I was wrong about that if he wants to see me again so soon.* What a bloody mess.

She inhaled a shuddering breath and took another sip of her drink. Pushing Donald aside for a moment, she decided to give herself time to reflect on how to handle him by ringing her mother first.

Her mother picked up the phone after the first ring. "Hello, darling. You read my mind, I was just going to ring you back. How are you?"

Sara smiled. Hearing her mother's warm, loving voice instantly calmed her anxieties, the way it always did. "I'm fine, Mum. How are you and Dad diddling?"

Her mother chuckled. "I love that word, it tickles me. Your father is behaving himself and doing as he's told at the moment. Listening to the doctor's advice, and when he slips up, he then has to listen to my nagging. Either way, he's taking it easier. Pottering around in the garden, nothing too stressful."

"Has he had any problems with his breathing over the last few days?"

"No, thankfully. I'm keeping a close eye on him. We have an appointment with the heart specialist in a fortnight."

"Let's hope they'll have some good news for him then. Keep the faith until then and ensure he doesn't overdo things. Knowing Dad and his wilfulness, I can appreciate that you're going to have a tough task on your hands there. He's not listening to this conversation, is he?"

"No. He's watering the back garden. I need to call on all my resources to fight his determination at times but I'll win the battles in the end, you can be sure of that, love. How's work going?"

Sara sighed. "Okay. Something came up today that I really think you should be aware of."

"Oh Lordy. What is it, now that you've scared me half to death?"

"Don't even joke about that, Mum. Are you sitting down?"

"Yes, I'm in the lounge. Whatever is the matter, child?"

"I don't want to cause you any concern; however, I'm only telling you this because you live rurally and should be aware of what has happened."

"Now you really are worrying me. This is so unlike you to be concerned about something, dear. What's wrong?"

"Please, promise me you won't fly off the handle and worry about this constantly?"

"How can I promise that when I haven't got a clue what you're going on about? Tell me, for goodness' sake, child. Don't you think we've gone through enough over the past few years, what with having to deal with Philip's death...I'm sorry, I shouldn't have brought that up."

"No need to apologise, Mum. If anything, it's because of Philip's death that I'm cautiously telling you about this."

Her mother gasped. "That sounds mighty ominous. Just tell me, dear. Stop keeping me in suspense."

"This morning, although it seems a hell of a lot longer than that—it's been a really long day of chasing our tails."

"Sara, stop going around the houses and spit it out. The more you delay telling me, the more anxious I'm becoming."

"Sorry, it's not intentional. Brace yourself, Mum. This morning I was called out to a scene in Bodenham."

"I see. What type of scene, love?"

"A murder scene, Mum."

Her mother fell silent on the other end of the line. No sharp intakes of breath, nothing.

"Mum, are you all right?"

"What? Oh my. I'm having trouble letting that sink in. A murder you say? Are you saying that you think I'll know the victim?"

Damn, that thought never even crossed my mind. "Maybe. Umm... victims, Mum. A husband and wife."

"Oh no. That's dreadful. Who?"

"A Ted and Maureen Flowers, do you know them?"

"I'll have to think about that. I don't recall the names. Murdered? I haven't seen anything about it on the news, love."

"I'm holding a press conference in the morning. It'll be all over the news then. The only reason I'm being so open with you about this is because I want to ensure you and Dad are extra vigilant going forward. Make sure you double-check the doors are locked at night. Dad put up a security light in the back garden, didn't he?"

"He did. Oh my. Was it a burglary that got out of hand?"

"We're not sure at this point, Mum. There was no sign of forced entry from what we could see, so who knows? Can you get Dad to install a light above the front door? If only to appease me?"

"I'll get him on to that ASAP. We'll take a run into Hereford in the morning to B&Q, see what they've got in stock. Whatever next? A murder—two murders—right on our doorstep. I'm not sure I'll be able to sleep at night now. Hey, never mind about us, we have each other, what about you? You're there all alone."

"Don't worry about me, Mum. I live on a small estate, nothing like that will happen around here. It's you two I'm more concerned about. I'll see if I can have a word with the desk sergeant in the morning, see if he has a sheet about 'security in the home' lying around. I know we used to do a regular leaflet drop now and again when I was stationed in Liverpool. I guess they've never felt the need for that type of thing around here. Well, times are changing."

"Don't say it like that. Let's hope this is a one-off. I think your father and I are pretty tight with our security measures anyway. We don't want to distract you from your enquiries. Do you have any clues as to who would commit this dreadful crime?"

"Not yet, Mum. Carla and I have spent the day questioning the family members. It's been a really tough, emotional day."

"Sorry to hear that, love. Did it bring back unwanted memories?"

Sara smiled. Her mother really did know her well. "Yes and no. When I first saw the pool of blood in the couple's residence, I managed to push it aside and deal with it in the end. I don't suppose I'll ever really get over what happened to Philip." Her eyes pricked with threatening tears.

"It's still less than two years, dear. These things take time. You know we're always on the end of the phone, don't you?"

"I appreciate that, Mum."

"Have Philip's parents stayed in touch with you?"

"Yes. Charlotte rings me once a month, pleads with me to go over there to see them. Crikey, as if I haven't got enough on my plate as it is. It's all right for her, she's a lady who lunches, has several hours in her day that she needs to fill. That luxury evades me."

"You should keep in touch with them all the same, love. I'm sure they appreciate how busy you are, we do."

"I'll give her a ring in the next few days. I think I'm going to be super busy on this case once we hit the ground with it."

"I'll keep my fingers crossed that you apprehend the person who carried out this brutal crime soon."

Sara inwardly laughed at her mother's choice of words that were straight out of the pages of the police handbook. "That's the plan, Mum. Would it be all right to invite myself for Sunday lunch this week?"

"Any time you want to come over here is fine by me. I'll nip into the supermarket while we're in town tomorrow and pick up a nice piece of beef, how's that?"

"Perfect, roast beef and Yorkshire pudding, just what the doctor ordered."

"Ha, not your father's doctor. He'll have to skip the Yorkshires this week."

"Oh no, we can't do that to him. If he's not allowed to have them it wouldn't hurt us giving them a miss, too, for once."

"We'll see."

"Thanks for the chat, Mum. Take care. See you around eleven on Sunday?"

"That's a date. It should be me telling you to take care, not the other way around."

"I'm always careful out there. Love you. Give Dad a hug from me."

"I will." Her mother blew a kiss down the phone and then hung up.

Sara felt a little guilty causing her mother to worry, although she'd rather be safe than sorry if there was a maniac on the loose. She jumped off the couch and made sure both the back and the front doors were properly secured then switched on the outside light as an added precaution. With her security measures in place, she returned to her seat and patted her lap for Misty to join her.

Stroking her cat instantly calmed her. After a while, Misty started kneading her leg, now and then catching her skin with her claws. She was tempted to push Misty onto the couch beside her, but the comfort her cat was bringing proved to be too overwhelming to ignore. She placed her head against the back of the sofa and closed her eyes, stroking Misty with one hand while holding her glass with the other.

The sound of the phone disturbed her chill time. She glanced down at the caller ID and instantly bit her lip, debating whether she should let the call get picked up by the voicemail for the second time that evening. *Coward! I'm going to have to speak to him sooner or later. Why not now?* Listening to her inner voice had the desired effect, and she punched the call answer button. "Hello."

"Oh, you are there. I was just about to hang up. How are you, Sara?"

"Hi, Donald. Sorry, I've only just got in. It's been a long day at work."

"No, it should be me apologising to you. Go, do what you need to do, I'll ring back later."

Guilt tugged at her heartstrings. "Honestly, it's no bother. I ate at lunchtime with my partner, so I don't have to prepare a meal or anything as boring as that."

"How have you been since we last met?"

She detected the hesitancy in his voice. "Busy," she replied nonchalantly, hoping to give him the impression that what had happened between them hadn't had a lasting consequence on her when it clearly had.

He laughed. "Ditto. We have the end of the financial year to get in order for all of our clients."

Donald was an accountant. Sara couldn't think of anything more boring than sitting at a desk all day number crunching. Saying that, Donald had never given her the impression that he was boring in the slightest. At least he didn't drone on and on about his work at any family gatherings she had attended. "I suppose we all have our crosses to bear."

"We do. It must be hard for you chasing people with outstanding parking fines to pay."

Sara just managed to stop herself spitting out the sip of vodka she'd taken. "Not sure where you get that idea from. Actually, it's been a pretty full-on day dealing with a murder enquiry."

He whistled down the line, almost deafening her. "Get you. Are you winding me up? Nothing that exciting goes on around here in sluggish Herefordshire."

"No, I'm not in the habit of winding people up in that way. I'm deadly serious, excuse the pun. If you must know, my partner and I have been comforting the victims' family all day," she snapped back. She bit down on her tongue after she'd finished her mini rant.

"Whoa! Okay, I didn't mean to cause offence."

"No. I'm sorry for snapping. I'm tired and I suspect I have a very taxing week ahead of me. What is it you wanted, Donald?"

He was silent for a moment, then finally said, "I was hoping we could go out to dinner one night?"

"Why?" she asked, her tone clipped.

"Does there have to be a reason why I want to see you?"

Sara puffed out her cheeks, unsure how to respond without hurting him. She shrugged as if he were sitting in the room with her.

"Sara?" he prompted quietly.

"It's too soon, Donald."

"Really? It's been over a year, almost two…Philip wouldn't want you to go into your shell like this."

She shook her head. No one had known Philip as well as she had. His family might think they had, but they hadn't. She and her husband had shared intimate secrets about each other that no one else was aware of. That kind of love and intimacy only came along once in someone's life. It could never be repeated, not in her eyes, and especially not with her husband's brother.

"You've gone quiet on me again. Speak to me," Donald insisted.

"I can't. Look, the last thing I want is for us to fall out. Philip and I had something special that I believe could never be replicated."

"You won't know unless you try," he persisted.

"As I've already told you, Donald, I'm not ready. I'm not sure I ever will be ready to move on. Your brother meant the world to me." She could feel herself becoming overwhelmed with emotion again. Why? Why should she have to justify the way she felt?

"I'm sorry. The last thing I wanted to do was upset you, Sara. Will you forgive me?"

"There's really nothing to forgive. Philip was the love of my life. My heart shattered into tiny pieces the day he was gunned down in front of me. That type of thing sometimes takes an eternity to overcome."

He fell silent for a while to the point Sara thought he was no longer on the line. "What was that about last week then? The kiss we shared."

Unexpected tears filled her eyes and dripped onto her cheeks. "Honestly? I don't know. That's the best I can do right now excuse-wise. I need to go, Donald."

"Okay. I'll ring you soon, if I have your permission?"

"If you want to, as long as you realise there are no guarantees."

"I get that. We can still be friends though, right?"

"Of course. Speak soon." She ended the call before they started going around in circles. She'd learnt over the years that Donald wasn't the type to take no for an answer. The thing was, he'd have to in this case.

Needing a distraction, she switched on the TV and flicked through the channels. Soaps and more damn soaps. Not for the first time she regretted not having Sky and the hundreds of channels available to choose from. But then that all came at a cost that she couldn't afford on her meagre wage. Everyone thought inspectors were highly compen-sated for the job they performed. Unfortunately, that could be nothing further from the truth. No, that was being unfair. Yes, an inspector's wage was adequate enough; her problem was that there was only one wage coming into the house. The council tax alone was now a stag-gering ten percent of her salary, which was outrageous. No doubt other people in the county were infuriated as much as she was. The trouble was, where would the price rise end?

With the amount of new-builds being erected, surely the rates should be going down not rising by three to six percent every year for the councils to waste on plush desks for their offices.

Sara downed her drink to get rid of the sour taste that had developed in her mouth. She continued to channel-hop and finally stumbled across a David Attenborough documentary about the Arctic. His voice was so soothing to her ear that it wasn't long before she dozed off on the couch. She woke to find the end credits filling the screen.

After letting Misty out and waiting for her to do her business, she bolted the back door again. Her beloved cat ran ahead of her upstairs to bed. Sara set the alarm for seven and switched off the light. Sleep evaded her for hours as her mind refused to let go of the day's events— all of them, including the conversation she'd had with her brother-in-law.

Eventually she drifted off, only to wake in a cold sweat after reliving the nightmare that had haunted her every night since Philip had died. Reaching for her mobile that she always kept on the bedside table, she replayed the voicemail message she refused to get rid of.

"Hello, darling. I'm running a little late. I'll be with you in five. Love you to the moon and back."

She sobbed the way she always did when she heard his melodious tone. She missed him so much. In the beginning, not long after he'd died in her arms, she had contemplated taking her own life just to be with him again. He truly had been her soul partner, and she craved every day to feel his arms wrapped around her. Now and again she was positive she'd heard him call her name or touched her arm. Up until now, she'd never revealed that to anyone, not even her mother.

She switched on the light again and picked up the small wedding photo she kept on her bedside table. She ran a finger around Philip's handsome features and then kissed the photo, wishing, not for the first time, that he was lying there in the bed beside her.

"I miss you so much. My heart will always remain broken until I join you."

A sudden gust of wind lifted the curtain. Instead of feeling concerned or nervous, she felt protected, as if Philip was in the room with her.

"Goodnight, my love."
She listened, expecting to hear a response.
Nothing came.

CHAPTER 8

Sara stretched out and stroked Misty. Her beloved cat purred loudly and lazily strode towards her and hopped onto her stomach. "Cheeky! Only a small cuddle, then I'll have to get up."

Her mind wandered back to the telephone call she'd received from Donald the previous evening. She didn't want to hurt his feelings; however, she sensed that was the direction she'd need to go to resolve the stalemate between them.

Sleep had evaded her most of the night—not the best preparation she could think of when in the throes of beginning a new case. "Right, time to get up, little one."

Her alarm sounded. She switched it off and rushed into her en suite. Ten minutes later, she emerged feeling fresher, although one look in the mirror told her that she appeared to be anything but refreshed. She withdrew a navy skirt suit and pink blouse from her wardrobe. Once dressed, she hurried downstairs to fix herself some coffee and toast.

Misty sauntered down the stairs a few minutes later. Sara let her companion out into the garden and waited at the back door for her to do her business. Misty returned, looking for her breakfast, and jumped up on the counter. "Oh no you don't. You know I hate it when you do that. On the floor where you belong, Munchkin."

After topping up Misty's bowl, Sara gathered her keys and handbag and set off for work. Walking into the incident room, she found Carla already at her desk, beavering away. "Bloody hell! You're putting me to shame. Two mornings on the trot you've beaten me into work. Everything all right?"

"Yep. Andrew is still away. I didn't sleep much last night, so instead of lying there doing bugger all, I decided to come in early instead."

"That makes two of us."

"What? You had trouble sleeping, too?"

Sara nodded and rolled her eyes. "Some cases play on the mind more than others, I suppose," she added swiftly, trying to avoid some of the questions she sensed coming her way, judging by the expression on her partner's face. "Coffee? Damn, I forgot to ring the vending machine people."

"Never say no to a surplus amount of coffee first thing. I'll make a note to ring them at nine."

"You're a gem." She handed her partner a coffee and went into her office to tackle the daily grind of post opening that proceeded everything in an inspector's life. It was the only downside of the job in her eyes. There was no point complaining about it, no one listened anyway. By all accounts, DCI Price was always anchored to her desk with far more paperwork to handle in a day than Sara had to contend with in a week. She had counted her blessings on that score more than once.

Not long after, Carla knocked on the door and stuck her head into the office. "Bad news, boss."

Sara glanced up and frowned. "Go on."

"I've just received a call about another double murder."

Sara threw herself back in the chair. "What? Where?"

"Canon Pyon."

"Not far from Bodenham as far as I can remember, right?"

Carla nodded. "That's right."

"Shit. Okay, we're going to be up against time this morning. I've got the press conference at eleven, it's not as if I can wriggle out of that. Damn! Are you ready to shoot off?"

"Ready when you are."

Sara pushed her paperwork aside, removed her jacket from the back of the chair and left the office with Carla. The rest of the team were sitting at their desks and acknowledged her the minute they saw her.

"Morning, all. I take it Carla has brought you up to date? We're going to shoot over to the scene now. I want you all to concentrate on the other case we're dealing with. The roundup I was intending to go through this morning regarding the Flowers' case will have to wait for now. We'll be back soon."

Sara and Carla left the room and rushed down the stairs and out of the entrance to Sara's vehicle.

Sara's mind was full of questions during the journey, the main one being whether they were dealing with a serial killer on their patch. The clear answer to that was yes, if they could prove the same person had committed both double murders. She struck the heel of her hand on the steering wheel when the traffic came to a grinding halt ahead of her. "Bloody roadworks. We could do without this today."

"I know a shortcut," Carla said. "You'll need to turn around and go up the Roman Road, though."

"Easily done." She switched on her siren to get out of the tiny space she was trapped in. A few of the cars in front pulled over to the side, allowing her the chance to squeeze out of the now enlarged gap. Carla held her hand up when a car coming in the opposite direction blasted its horn as Sara did a U-turn in the road.

Carla gave her instructions which turning to take, and Sara navigated the narrow lanes with ease while still keeping up her speed. She emerged onto the A49 minutes later and let out a sigh of relief. "I'll have to remember that route in the future. Still struggling with finding the shortcuts needed to navigate this city. Glad to have you by my side."

"You'll get used to it. I'm surprised you don't know about that route, you could use it to get you home earlier at night."

Arriving at the scene, Sara spotted the pathologist's vehicle and a SOCO van. "We'd better don our suitable clothing before we feel Lorraine's wrath."

They flashed their IDs at the uniformed officer, and he raised the crime scene tape high enough for them to duck under. Entering the house, it didn't take long for Sara to work out that a struggle had taken place. Most of the furniture in the lounge had been upended.

"Hi, you two. Glad you could join us," Lorraine smiled and then shook her head. "Looks like the killer has upped his game on this one."

"You think it's the same culprit?" Sara asked, surveying the room.

"Don't you?" Lorraine asked, surprise resonating in her tone. "Two double murders in the space of twenty-four to forty-eight hours, depending on the time of the deaths, which I've yet to determine."

"Granted. I was hoping that wouldn't be the case. Ignore me, rough night."

Lorraine eyed her with concern for a moment or two as if expecting her to divulge why she'd had a rough night. When Sara didn't respond, she said, "My first reaction would be that we're dealing with the same person. This time he didn't hold back. The Flowers got off light compared to this couple."

"Do we have a name for the victims?" Carla asked.

"Linda and Samuel Meredith. Both in their late sixties, relative youngsters compared to the Flowers," Lorraine told them, sadness shrouding her features.

"Who found them?" Sara asked, walking across the room to the hallway. "Are the vics in the bedroom?"

"Yes. The culprit did the same, dragged both of them through the house. To answer your first question, the neighbour came over first thing. She heard a scream last night but neglected to do anything about it as it was too dark to investigate. She lives by herself and was scared. At first light, she came to the house and found the front door unlocked. She opened the door, saw the mess the place was in and called 999 immediately. She's beside herself."

"To be expected. We'll have a chat with her after we've had a good look around. I can't be here too long, I have a press conference booked in for eleven."

"No problem. I'll do my thing here and send you over my report ASAP. I'll show you into the bedroom."

Lorraine led the way up the narrow hallway to a large double bedroom at the rear. They passed another bedroom on the right. Peering into the room, Sara noticed the bed was unmade. *Maybe the couple slept in separate rooms.*

They entered the main bedroom to yet more carnage. It was clear the culprit was intent on finding something he thought the couple were hiding. "Was he searching for money?"

Lorraine shrugged. "Perhaps. Either way, I think he tortured the couple for a few minutes before they died, possibly to try and get the truth out of them." The couple were sitting on the floor, back to back. They had a tow rope tied around their chests, joining them together. Their clothing was blood-soaked, and all around them the carpet was stained with their blood.

Sara gulped, memories she had stored away for a while suddenly emerging. She drew her gaze away from the tragic couple and caught Carla eyeing her with concern.

"Are you all right?" asked her partner.

"Fine. Shocked, that's all." She walked through the room and bent down to see if there was anything lurking under the bed. The space was empty. "Nothing under the bed. Was there anything there to begin with? Did the killer find something of use?"

"Why look there in the first place?" Carla asked.

"I'm putting myself into the mindset of the victims. My grandparents always kept anything they deemed important under their bed. I just presumed everyone of an older generation did the same. Bearing in mind the Flowers kept their money under a loose floorboard beneath their bed."

"Good point. That fact momentarily slipped my mind," Carla replied, her cheeks flaring up in embarrassment.

Sara winked at her. "So, you reckon he tortured the woman first, trying to get the man to divulge where their loot was hidden?"

"That's my take on things," Lorraine agreed.

"What? And he killed them both once he'd found what he was searching for?"

Lorraine shrugged. "Your guess is as good as mine. I suppose only a family member will be able to answer that."

"Twisted bastard either way. The couple must have really suffered during their ordeal, judging by the amount of blood."

"He stabbed them repeatedly. Sliced off the man's ear." Lorraine pointed at the bloody body part lying a few feet away that Sara had neglected to see.

She sighed. "That's sad. To feel the need to mutilate someone like that. Horrendous."

"I agree. I'm going to get on now, if there's nothing else you need from me."

"Don't let us hold you up. We'll have a brief look around the lounge and then go and see what the neighbours have to say."

Sara and Carla left Lorraine and her team in the bedroom. On the way back down the hallway, Sara paused at the doorway to the other bedroom, noting the girly contents of the room. "My guess is the wife probably slept in here."

"I think you're right. Time's marching on, boss. We've got the roadworks to contend with on the way back, remember."

"And your shortcut to take if necessary. One more stop, and then we'll make a move. Get on to the station for me. Organise a team of uniformed officers to come out here and do the initial house-to-house enquiries for us this time. We'll be too busy."

Carla withdrew her phone from her pocket and contacted the station as instructed. Sara paused at the front door and decided to call at the house opposite first.

A woman in a thick woollen cardigan opened the door. "Hello, there. I'm DI Sara Ramsey, and this is my partner, DS Carla Jameson. Are you the neighbour who called 999?"

"I am. Do you want to come in? It's a little nippy out there today. Or is it just me and the shock setting in?"

Sara smiled. "Thank you. It is a little fresh. Sorry, I didn't catch your name."

"Barbara Knott. Linda was one of my closest friends. I shall miss her dearly. Damn, I've been trying hard all morning not to break down, and now look at me. Come through to the lounge, the gas fire is on in there. Sorry, where are my manners? Do you want a drink?"

"No, we're fine."

They walked into the brightly coloured lounge with its modern furniture. The whole ensemble shocked Sara.

"I know. It's a bit garish. My daughter came over last month, insisted that I needed a makeover, and this was the result. She's delighted with it. I neither like nor dislike it."

Sara smiled. "Definitely a style that would take some getting used to."

"My worry is that she's threatening to come over and do the rest of the house. How on earth I'm going to deter her from doing that I'm at a loss to know. Anyway, enough about my problems, which are insignificant in the grand scheme of things. How can I help to catch the warped bastard who has done this to my friends?"

"We're sorry for your loss. It must have been a shock to have discovered your friends like that."

"It was. That image will remain with me the rest of my damn life, I can tell you. Please, take a seat. At least the couch is comfy."

The three of them sat. Carla withdrew her notebook and began to take notes while Sara asked the woman what she knew. "Maybe you could run through what happened."

"It was around ten or ten-fifteen last night. That's right, the News at Ten had just started. I thought I heard a scream outside, in the distance. I immediately muted the TV, but then everything sounded as it should, silent. We don't tend to get a lot of noise out here at night. Most of the residents are of an older generation and respectful. It's not like living on a new estate."

"Okay. So you didn't leave your property to investigate the noise?"

"No. I would never open my door, not at that time of night.

Although, I'm regretting not doing that now. Perhaps if I'd rung the police last night, you might have caught the person responsible."

"Please, don't feel guilty. There's really no need."

Barbara inhaled a shuddering deep breath before she continued, "I had a restless night last night and was up at the crack of dawn. It doesn't help with these bright mornings—I've not had a lie-in lately. I didn't even have a cup of tea. I went straight over to Linda and Samuel's house. The front door was ajar, so I pushed it open to find the place all topsy-turvy. My heart sank instantly. I knew something dreadful had happened. I called out to them both but didn't receive a response. I tiptoed through the house, calling their names in case they were in the bathroom or bedroom. That's when I found them." Tears spilled onto her cheeks. She sniffled and wiped her nose with a hanky. "I'm sorry. I've never seen a dead person before. It's affected me badly to see my friends slaughtered like that. Why? Who would do such a callous thing? Rob innocent people of their lives like that?"

"That's what we intend to find out, Barbara. I'm sorry you discovered your friends in such a way."

"I'll never recover. I'm going to put the house on the market today. I can't stay around here knowing that there is a killer on the loose. I could be next on his hit list."

"Maybe take a few days to consider your options. Can you stay with your daughter for a while?"

"I've rung her. I have an agent coming around later this morning, and then my daughter is going to come by this afternoon to pick me up. If I stayed around here, I would never sleep again. I'd be constantly listening out for strange noises, signs of someone about to break in. Why do you think this happened?"

"We have no idea on that at present. I have to ask if either Linda or Samuel confided in you that they had possibly fallen out with someone recently."

She shook her head and wiped her nose again. "They weren't the type. Everyone in this community looks out for each other. We're all friendly, not a baddun amongst us. Not a lot of villages or communities can brag about that these days."

Sara smiled. "You're right. Do the Merediths have any family? Maybe a relative who lives close by."

Barbara gasped and covered her mouth with her hand. She shook her head slowly then dropped her hand again. "Oh my. The thought never entered my mind. Geraldine...they have a daughter. She lives with them."

Sara thought back to the spare room she had spotted. "Was Geraldine in the house at the time, do you know?"

"She's always here. The poor girl has special needs."

Sara's heart sank. If Geraldine wasn't here, then where was she? Had the killer abducted her? Killed her and left her body in a ditch somewhere for them to find? "I need to go back to the house to obtain a photo, Carla. You stay here and question Barbara." Sara raced out of the house and back across the road, the white suit she was wearing rustling as she moved. "Lorraine, Lorraine, are you there?"

The pathologist emerged from the hallway wearing a frown. "What on earth is the matter?"

"The couple had a daughter living with them. Have you found any signs of a struggle in the other bedroom?"

"Shit, shit, shit! No. Bloody hell, you don't think the bastard has got her, do you?"

Sara nodded slowly. "I do. Damn, she's got special needs, Lorraine."

"Fuck. That's all we need. Her in the hands of a frigging maniac."

Sara glanced around the room from the doorway, not wishing to step back into the house in case she contaminated the scene. "I need to find a photo of the girl. Please, help me look for one."

Lorraine went to the bookcase, and beneath it, lying on the floor alongside all the books that had been dislodged from the shelf, was a picture frame. "I've got one."

She crossed the room and handed the frame to Sara. "Damn. I hope we bloody find her soon before it's too late. Shite! She's got Down's syndrome." She shook her head as the shock of the situation overwhelmed her.

Lorraine rested a hand on her forearm. "Sara, you can do this. You need to put this aside and think of her as any other person who has gone missing."

Sara flung her arms out to the side. "How can you say that? I know deep down that I'm not going to be able to do that. Fuck! What does this guy want?"

Lorraine issued her a weak smile and shrugged. "The signs are far from clear on this one. Again, up until now, we've not come across anything useful DNA-wise."

Sara pointed at her. "See, now that's what convinces me that this guy knows what he's doing. I wonder if he knew the Merediths had a daughter living with them. Jesus! What if he kills her?"

Lorraine worriedly ran a hand around her face. "What you need to consider is that up to this point, he had the opportunity to kill her and hasn't. I think we need to take heart from that."

Sara nodded. "I hear you. What if he has killed her, taken her body with him with the intention of dumping her somewhere? How do we know he's not playing games with us? What a frigging mess. Why me? Why on my patch? The damn press are going to love this!"

"You're talking nonsense. Stop taking this personally, Sara."

Sara sucked in a breath then let it out slowly, lowering her head to her chest. "Maybe. Shit! What do I know about what kind of needs this woman has?"

"I don't know either. You're going to need to seek expert advice on that one."

"You're right. I better shoot off. I need to get back to the station. Do your best—I know you always do, but please, I'm begging you and your team to be extra vigilant on this one."

"Don't worry about that. We'll go over this place with a magnifying glass if we need to. I want this fucker caught as much as you do."

Sara walked back to her car, removed her paper suit and jumped into the driver's seat, contemplating what she should do next. Carla emerged from the neighbour's house, disrobed and sat in the seat next to her.

Sara placed a call to the station. "Jill, it's me." She inhaled then exhaled a large breath. "We've got a tough one here. Another double murder. Carla and I are on our way back to the station now. I need you to do some research for me, if you would?"

"What do you need, boss?" Jill replied.

"I want you to find out what special needs someone with Down's syndrome has." Sara sensed Carla's head sharply turn her way. She held up a finger as if to say, 'I'll fill you in later', then continued, "Do they take special medication? Do they require a special diet perhaps? You get the gist."

"I'll get onto it right away, boss."

"Thanks. See you soon, Jill." Sara jabbed a finger at her phone to end the call.

"Why did you want to know that?" Carla asked.

"Because Geraldine Meredith is Down's, and it looks like the bastard has abducted her."

Carla bashed her clenched fist against the dashboard. "Fucking shit, that's all we sodding need. Christ, you better hold me back when we eventually catch up with this shit."

"I think you'll need to join a long line of people who'll be wanting to dish out punishment on this one, Carla. Christ, I feel sick. That poor woman. She's going to feel lost and alone, confused, and Lord knows what other emotions will be running through her if she bloody witnessed the deaths of her parents."

"Don't, it doesn't bear thinking about. Let's go. This case has just notched up a little to a must-solve-swiftly case. I hope for his sake he doesn't hurt her. I don't profess to know what goes on in some of these bastards' twisted minds."

Sara nodded. "I agree. Let's not dwell on that side of things. Think positively. We *will* get her back unharmed. Damn, I should've asked Jill to put out a missing person alert for Geraldine." Sara reached in the back seat for the photo she had thrown there. "Take a photo on your phone and ring Jill back for me. The sooner we get that actioned, the better." She started the engine and put her foot down in her haste to get back to the station in record time, whether there were roadworks in the way or not.

CHAPTER 9

He paced the floor in front of the frightened woman. Her eyes were bulbous with fear. She stared at him, making him feel uncomfortable under her gaze. *What the fuck was I thinking about taking her? I should have killed her along with her parents.* The truth was, he couldn't bring himself to do it.

Running a hand through his short black hair, he secured her to the bed. She didn't attempt to fight him or struggle against her confines in the slightest. She just continued to stare at him confused.

He rushed downstairs and rummaged in the fridge. There were a couple of eggs in there, a few tomatoes and a manky pepper that should have been destined for the bin. Instead, he chopped up the tomatoes and pepper, beat the eggs with the last drop of milk in the carton and placed it all in a pan. Omelettes were the only decent meal he had the aptitude to muster up at short notice for the woman.

After ten minutes, he plated up the omelette that had split when he'd tried to get it out of the pan. He took it upstairs and handed it to her, pleased with himself that he'd shown a willingness to care for her properly, even if he had tied one of her hands to the bed. "Eat. You must be hungry."

Her gaze drifted from him to the plate he was holding and then back up to him. Slowly, she shook her head. In the hours he'd held her captive, she hadn't spoken a single word. He had no idea if she could even speak.

He forced the plate under her nose, hoping the smell would entice her to pick up the fork. It didn't. She simply stared at him with those large, lost eyes. Her expression cut him, tore his insides apart. He'd killed five people in the last forty-eight hours and only felt a smattering of guilt, but having this woman stare at him like this was tearing him to shreds. "Please, eat. You need to keep your strength up. I promise, I'm not going to hurt you. Eat."

She shook her head slightly and gently pushed the plate away with her free hand. "No. Not hungry. I want my mummy."

Unexpected tears pricked his eyes. *What the fuck have I done?* "I'm sorry," he muttered, feeling genuine guilt for the first time since his quest had begun.

"Want my mummy."

"I'm sorry. Eat the damn omelette. You need to keep your strength up."

She shook her head and squeezed her lips tightly together.

He gave up, sat on the bed beside her and tucked into the omelette himself. Out of the corner of his eye, he saw the woman watching him place every mouthful in his mouth. Once or twice he offered her a bite —she refused each time.

After he'd finished, he took the plate downstairs and boiled the kettle. He kicked himself when he realised he'd used the last of the milk in the omelette. He put on his jacket and left the house. The corner shop at the end of the street was handy for what he needed. He bought two pints of milk when he usually opted for a single pint. He returned to the house and continued to make the coffee for two people, in the hope the woman would relent and at least have a drink with him.

He returned upstairs and offered her the mug of coffee. She made no attempt to take it from him. Instead, she turned her face away to stare at the wall beside her.

"Please. You have to drink. I mean you no harm."

She faced him and said only one sentence, "I want my mummy."

He threw his mug against the wall and instantly regretted his actions when she curled into a ball beside him and rocked back and forth. She was crying, large tears. As each one fell, his heart squeezed a little more. He was at a loss what to say or do next so left the room.

He paced the lounge downstairs, pondering what his next move should be. He was light by nine and a half grand. He'd need to make another hit before Friday. Two days to source another victim and come up with the goods. He flipped through the Flowers' address book for more of their friends who lived locally.

CHAPTER 10

Sara and Carla made it back to base by the skin of their teeth. Sara ran through the station, stopping off at the loo to assess herself. She ran a comb through her hair and came to the conclusion that she looked half-decent. Then she left Carla to fill in the rest of the team while she ran back down the stairs and into the press room. Outside the room, she was surprised to see DCI Carol Price pacing the area.

"Crikey, you've only just made it."

"Ma'am. Sorry, we had another murder scene to attend to this morning."

"Crap. I hadn't heard. Are you going to mention that one at the same time? Is there a connection, do you think?"

"Hard to discount a connection when both incidents happened within a few miles of each other, ma'am. There's something else."

DCI Price inclined her head. "Quickly, we don't have much time, what is it?"

"The latest victims had a daughter, ma'am. She was missing from the residence when we got there."

"Damn! So, what's his intention, to demand a ransom?"

Sara shrugged. "Possibly. The thing is, ma'am, the woman has Down's syndrome."

DCI Price immediately slapped her hand against her forehead. "You're kidding me?"

"Sorry, ma'am, I would never joke about something as grave as this."

"Shit! I know you wouldn't. Do you want to postpone the press conference?"

"No, ma'am. I need it to go ahead as planned. I also think I should mention the latest crime plus Geraldine's abduction. The trouble with that is, I haven't had the time to track down any relatives of the latest couple."

"Then you know as well as I do that you can't mention it. Not without contacting the relatives first."

Sara nodded and sighed. "I know that, ma'am. Is there any way I can mention that Geraldine is missing? Forget I said that, I know what your response is going to be."

"Exactly. You can't possibly inform the public before we've contacted the relatives. Maybe get one of your team on that now, and you'll have to call another conference tomorrow."

"Carla is looking into it now, ma'am. The last thing I want to do is hold another conference within a few days. I have four murders to solve. I don't have the time to deal with the press more than once per case. I'm worried about Geraldine and her safety though, ma'am."

"So am I. Have you issued a missing person alert on her?"

"Yes, I did that about an hour ago. Bugger, this case or cases are driving me to distraction already, and they've only just begun."

"Stick with it, Inspector. My door is always open if you need to run anything by me. I'll be sure to keep on top of my paperwork just in case you need me to lend a hand."

"Thanks. I think I'm going to need all the support I can get on this one."

"That goes without saying. You're capable of handling this case, I've got no qualms about that. Just don't be afraid to ask for help."

"I won't. We better go in—that is if you're going to join me?"

"That's why I'm here. Let's do this."

They both entered the medium-sized room that was full of press people from the two local TV stations and the local newspaper, plus there were also a few members of the press from neighbouring counties who usually joined the conferences.

Sara ran through what had happened to the Flowers and appealed for help from the general public. She omitted to mention any kind of reward the family were anxious to put forward at this stage, aware of the stress that would put her team under fielding such calls. In the past, any case with a reward attached had given the police a mountain to climb within hours of the appeal being aired. She needed to keep the information clean on this one, at least for the time being.

DCI Price allowed Sara to make the appeal, then she took over the responsibility of answering all the questions the press had concerning the couple's death.

An hour later, Sara and DCI Price thanked the press for attending and left the room. They ascended the stairs together. "Want me to come and have a chat with the team?"

"That's up to you, ma'am. Obviously, what with having to rush back to attend the press appeal, I haven't had time to bring the team up to date on the other case as yet."

"We can do that together, Sara."

She nodded, feeling appreciative of the DCI's support but couldn't help wondering if that would backfire on her later down the line.

The second they stepped into the office, Carla left her seat and headed towards the vending machine. "Coffee, ma'am?"

"That's very kind. Black, no sugar for me," DCI Price called back.

Sara nodded appreciatively at Carla. Seconds later, Carla handed them both a coffee. "The appeal went as well as expected. There's no need for me to tell you what to do regarding any information that comes in from that. Let's remain focussed on the two cases we're dealing with. Carla, any luck tracking down any relatives for the Merediths?"

"Still working on that one, boss. Nothing coming up so far."

"I don't suppose anyone has had eyes on Geraldine yet?"

Carla shook her head. "Again, nothing."

"Her safety is paramount. We need to ensure that is our priority at all times. I'll bring the board up to date in a while. I'll be in the office with DCI Price for the next few minutes. Interrupt us if any valuable information comes in."

"Will do, boss."

Sara led the way into her office, grateful that her desk was tidy at least, even if she hadn't had time to deal with her post first thing. She sat behind her desk and glanced up at DCI Price.

Her superior sat opposite her and took a sip of her coffee then placed the cup on the desk in front of her. "I wanted to have a brief chat with you."

"About the case, or should that be cases now, ma'am?"

"Indirectly, yes. Cards on the table. You know as well as I do, the reason behind your request for a transfer to this area was to get away from all the blood and gore in your previous division."

"That's right, ma'am, but I'm not following you. Sorry for being dense."

"You're far from dense, Inspector." She heaved out a breath. "I'm sorry, I'm failing to make myself clear here. What I'm trying to say in a clumsy way is, how are you doing under the pressure?" She pointed at Sara and wagged her finger when her mouth dropped open. "See, now wait, don't answer that, because it came out the wrong way again."

"I'm confused, ma'am. What exactly are you getting at? Are you insinuating that you think I'm not up to the job?"

DCI Price thumped her clenched fist against her temple. "No. See, I knew it would come out wrong. I'm not insinuating any such thing. What I'm trying to ascertain is if you're coping all right on a personal level."

"Ah, I see. Of course I am. I would never let the two collide, ma'am. It's been around nineteen months since Phil's death. I'm not saying that I don't think of him often, but I'm more than capable of continuing my role as inspector, if that's your concern."

"It's not. Damn. What I was getting at in my hapless way of going about things, is whether the brutality of the crimes is affecting you. As you know, we don't get a lot of heinous crimes such as this happening in our area."

"I know, ma'am. I hope the criminals in the area haven't cottoned on to my presence and decided to up the ante just because I'm now policing Hereford."

DCI Price laughed. "I hope you're wrong about that, too. If ever things become too much for you personally, you will let me know, right? I'd hate to see you crumble on the job."

Sara shook her head. "I'm not likely to do that, ma'am. I'm over his death," she lied.

DCI Price narrowed her eyes as if she was about to challenge her. Instead, she took another sip of her coffee. "All right, I'll give you the benefit of the doubt on that one. What are your plans re the cases?"

"I think the first thing we need to ascertain is whether the Flowers and the Merediths knew each other and go from there."

"Do you know what the motive is?"

"Initially I thought it was about money. At this time, we have no idea what has gone missing from the Merediths' house, apart from their daughter, that is. I'm finding it difficult to get my mind around that. Why would this person or persons take her?"

"You're assuming the killer or killers have taken her. What if she ran off? Have you considered that option?"

Sara shook her head. "I hadn't. I'll organise a search team just in case."

"I'm not suggesting you're wrong; however, it would be better to cover all the options from the get-go. What about the witnesses?"

"We had a neighbour at the first murder scene who saw a man standing outside the Flowers' front door on Saturday evening. Unfortunately, he didn't take much notice of the person because the Flowers had a lot of visitors."

"That's a shame. What about the second case?"

"The neighbour opposite heard a scream, but it was too dark for her to investigate. She called at the house the next day, found the front door ajar and discovered the couple dead in their bedroom. She called the police right away."

DCI Price sighed. "DNA or any form of evidence at either scene?"

"Nothing as yet. No, scrub that, we have a bloody trainer footprint at the Flowers' house. The pathologist reckons the imprint from the trainer is from an off-the-shelf shoe model that has probably been sold millions of times over the years."

"Not helping and exceedingly frustrating. Let's hope something comes in from the appeal regarding that. So, going forward, your main focus will be tracking down the family members and trying to locate the daughter, right?"

"That sums it up perfectly, ma'am. Obviously, any information we obtain from the appeal will go to the top of our list and will be actioned right away. Until then, we'll continue doing our background checks into the Flowers' family."

"You think one of them could be behind their murders?"

"The thought briefly crossed my mind; however, I think we can discount that theory given the other case dropping into our laps this morning."

"Maybe you shouldn't discount that theory too soon. What if the Flowers and Merediths were friends and the killer knew this?"

"Again, it's something we need to bear in mind, ma'am."

"Okay, I should get back to my laborious paperwork. Keep me informed every step of the way."

Sara rose from her seat and walked out of the office with DCI Price. "I will, ma'am."

After seeing the DCI to the door, she stopped by Carla's desk. "Any news on tracking down a family member yet?"

"I've got the name of an aunt. I haven't made contact as yet, thought you'd want to do that, boss." Her partner held out a sheet of paper with the name *Katherine Ross* written on it.

"I'll ring her now." Sara bypassed the vending machine, even though her need was great after the DCI's visit, and went into her office. She closed the door behind her.

She dialled the woman's number and waited anxiously as the

phone's dial tone sounded four times before it was answered. "Hello, is that Katherine Ross?"

"It is. Who wants to know? I've got double glazing, central heating and a new vacuum cleaner, so I'm not in the market for buying any of those, thank you."

"Don't hang up, Mrs Ross, please. I'm DI Sara Ramsey. I'm calling about Linda and Samuel Meredith."

"Okay, Linda is my sister. What about them?"

"I'd really rather not do this over the phone. Is there any chance I can come and see you?"

"That sounds ominous. Are they in trouble, Inspector?"

"Do you live far? Sorry, I don't have your address, only your phone number."

"I live on the outskirts of Hereford. What's this about? You're scaring me."

"In person, if you don't mind," Sara persisted. "I can be there within a few minutes."

"Very well. It's five Cotswold Lane, Upper Breinton."

"Thank you. Depending on the traffic, I should be there within twenty minutes."

"I'll see you then."

Sara hung up and raced around her desk, pulling on the jacket she had not long removed. "Carla, do you want to come with me? I'm going to see Mrs Ross in person; she doesn't live far."

Carla left her paperwork and followed Sara out of the incident room. "Makes sense to talk to her in person," Carla said, rushing to keep up with her.

"That's what I thought. I've never told a person that their loved ones had been murdered over the phone yet, and I don't intend to start now. It's just not how I do things."

CHAPTER 11

F ifteen minutes later, they drew up outside a quaint cottage in
the heart of the Herefordshire countryside. "It's beautiful out
here," Sara noted.

"My mum always said she'd want to retire out this way when the
time comes. There's a little known place down the road where you can
walk the dog along the banks of the River Wye."

"That sounds wonderful. I don't blame your mum wanting to move
here. Okay, here we go." Sara tapped the knocker to the front door. She
had her warrant card in her hand ready to show the woman the instant
the door was opened.

"Ah, you're on time. I do like people who stick to their word. Do
you have some form of ID? You can't be too careful these days."

"Indeed. Pleased to meet you, Mrs Ross." Sara flashed her ID.

Mrs Ross stood back to allow them access to a warm and cosy interior. She showed them into a lounge that was dominated by large
exposed beams and an inglenook fireplace which housed a wood-
burning stove.

"Please take a seat. Now what's all this about? I tried to ring Linda
after your call, but the phone rang and rang, which is unusual. One of
them always answers."

Sara smiled at the woman. "It is with the greatest regret that I have to tell you both Linda and Samuel died at their home this morning."

Katherine's hand covered her right cheek, and she shook her head, obviously stunned by the news. "What? How did they die? I only spoke to my sister a few days ago. She and Samuel were perfectly all right then."

"I'm sorry, but they were murdered."

"No! I don't believe this. How? No, forget I said that, I don't want the details. I mean, why them? How did someone get into their home?"

"We really can't give you any answers at present. We're dealing with a similar case in the same area. There will be an appeal going out on the evening news. We think the two cases are connected. Unfortunately, I didn't have the time to contact you before the appeal went out. Your sister and her husband won't be mentioned in that appeal; I wanted to inform you or any other relatives before you heard about it on the news."

She nodded. "I appreciate that. My God, wait...what about Geraldine? You haven't said anything about her. Is she also dead?"

"We don't believe so."

"What do you mean? Either she is or she isn't, which is it?"

"No. She wasn't at the house."

Katherine frowned and wrung her hands in her lap. "I don't understand. If she wasn't at the house, then where is she? This makes no sense at all."

"We don't have all the answers yet, I'm afraid. I'm aware that your niece has Down's syndrome. Can you tell me what special needs she has? Does she take medication every day, for instance?"

"My mind is all over the place. I can't get my head around all that you've told me. Wait, yes, she takes tablets every day because she has a heart defect."

Sara's pulse raced. "I suspected something along those lines. Okay, we need to do something drastic in that case, and you're going to have to help me, if you're up for that?"

"Anything. I just want my niece back home safely." She gasped.

"Oh no, you're not saying the person who killed my sister and her husband has taken her, are you?"

Sara shrugged. "We really don't know if that's the case or not. Do you think there is any way, given the opportunity, that Geraldine might have run off?"

"To be honest with you, no. Oh God, what if she saw Linda and Samuel? What if she was there to witness their deaths?" Large tears formed and dripped onto her cheeks. She wiped them away with a tissue she extracted from the box beside her.

"I'm sorry, I don't profess to know how difficult this must be for you. My suggestion would be that we should hold another urgent appeal with the media. I know it's a big ask in the circumstances, but I wondered if you'd be willing to sit alongside me during an appeal, to make a plea to the person who might have her. Maybe if they realise Geraldine needs constant supervision, they'll rethink their decision and let her go."

"What if they think the opposite and end her life, too? My God, what do I do for the best?"

"It will be a hard decision for you to make. I would go along the lines that if we pleaded with the person who might have her, he could very well let her go. Thinking logically, and we have to take heart from this, there must be a reason why he didn't kill Geraldine or leave her at the property."

"A killer with a conscience, is that what you're saying?"

Sara hitched up her shoulder. "I really can't answer that. What do you think? About the appeal, I mean."

"Of course I'll do it. I want my niece back and I'm prepared to do whatever it takes to get her back, Inspector."

"Can you give me five minutes to arrange everything?"

"Okay, would you like a drink in the meantime?" She rose to her feet, but her legs gave way beneath her, and she collapsed into her chair again. "I'm sorry. It appears the mind is willing, however, the body is unwilling to contribute."

"No problem. Carla, would you do the honours?"

Carla nodded and left the room. Sara stood in the bay window of the lounge, overlooking the woman's beautifully planted front garden to place the call to the station. It didn't take her long to emphasise the need with the press officer to hold another appeal so soon. Jane was confident she'd be able to pull it off because of what was at stake, probably by holding another appeal later on that afternoon. "Get back to me ASAP, if you would."

"I will," Jane replied before she ended the call.

Sara returned to her seat opposite Katherine. "I know what a shock all of this must be for you."

"It is, a great shock. Truthfully, I don't think I'm allowing it to fully sink in yet. I want my niece back safe and sound before I allow myself to crumble. You say this person has killed other people. Where? In Hereford itself?"

"On the other side of the city, in Bodenham. The other murders only happened yesterday, so we haven't really had a chance to begin our investigations as such. We're hoping that once the appeal goes out we'll be inundated with calls, giving us the leads we need to get the case started."

"It's a rarity around these parts, isn't it?"

"Totally. I thought I was coming to a quiet area when I transferred, where the only cases I would have to attend were a bit of sheep rustling or things along that line."

"Where have you transferred from?"

"Liverpool."

"Oh my. I have a nephew who lives in Bootle. He's always complaining about the gang culture up there and the drive-by shootings people have to contend with."

Sara felt the colour drain from her face.

"Oh dear, sorry, have I said something wrong? You look a little pale, Inspector."

"My husband was killed during a shootout. He died in my arms."

Unbeknown to Sara, Carla had stepped into the room carrying a tray. She gasped.

Sara closed her eyes, regretting her decision to open up to Katherine. She'd kept her secret from the rest of her team all these months and now she feared it would be all around the station within the next few days.

"I had no idea," Carla muttered, placing the tray of drinks on the coffee table.

"I'd prefer if that information remained between us, Sergeant."

"You have my word, boss."

"I'm sorry. I didn't mean to pry, Inspector, forgive me. So, you'll know exactly how numb I'm feeling right now," Katherine said.

"I do indeed. All I can say is that over time the numbness disperses. I still get days when I feel down, and the nightmares invade my sleep occasionally, like last night. But in the main, I cope. We have to carry on, don't we?"

"Did they ever find the person responsible?" Carla asked.

Sara shook her head and swallowed noisily. "No. Please, I'd rather not discuss the subject further. This isn't about me, it's about doing all we can to get Geraldine back, unharmed." Sara's mobile rang. She hopped out of her chair and went to the window again to answer the call. "Hi, Jane. How did you get on?"

"I had to beg, borrow and steal a time slot. They've all agreed to another appeal taking place at three this afternoon, and the good news is, they're going to edit the appeal of this morning to incorporate both cases."

"You're an absolute treasure. Thanks so much. I'll see you just before three then."

"Always a pleasure to help, you know that, Inspector."

"See you later." Sara ended the call and returned to her seat. Carla handed her a cup of coffee. Sara took a sip and confirmed the arrangements that Jane had made. "Will you be able to drive to the station this afternoon, Katherine, or would you rather me send a car to pick you up?"

"The last thing I want to do is put you out, but would you mind if someone picked me up? I'm not sure I can trust my legs to work well enough to drive at present after what happened a few moments ago."

"It's really not a problem. The appeal is booked for three. I'll send a driver to fetch you at two-thirty, if that's all right?"

"Perfect. I'm already getting nervous about being in front of the cameras. What if I mess things up?"

"You won't. I'll be right there beside you. I think the best way to overcome your nerves would be if you thought about the appeal as though you and I were having a chat, just as we are now. Ignore all the lights and the cameras. Do you think you'll be able to manage that?"

"I think so. We'll soon find out."

Sara smiled reassuringly at her. "You'll be fine. We'll drink this then get back to the station."

CHAPTER 12

He paced the floor, in two minds what to do for the best. He wanted to care for Geraldine, but she was refusing to eat or drink anything. He was aware that she needed to have regular sustenance. His sister had Down's; she died when she was seven. Not many people knew that about him. He loved his sister, her funny quirky ways. Most boys hated being around their sisters when they were in their teens, but he hadn't. He used to rush home from school every day to play with her. He loved the way she beamed at him the second he walked into the house. Sonia used to run into his arms, hugging the air out of his body with her fierce grip.

Staring at Geraldine made his heart lurch. He wanted so much to care for her. Guilt was guiding his every move right now. Had he known that the Merediths had a Down's daughter, he would never have gone near their place. All he wanted to do now was make amends for his actions. At the back of his mind, Mick's warning was prominent— he had three days to come up with twenty grand. That alone was enough to prompt what he was about to do next.

With Geraldine tied to the bed, he bent down and whispered, "I won't be long. You'll be safe here with me. Don't fight me, Geraldine.

I mean you no harm. I have to nip out for a moment or two. Do you want me to pick up some sherbet for you? Sonia used to like the way it tickled her tongue. Do you like it, too?"

Geraldine stared at him, neither affirming nor disagreeing with him. He smiled and squeezed her hand gently. She turned her head away from him. It was then that he realised she must be scared of the way he looked, the pasting Mick had given him. He touched his face and flinched when his hand swept over his bruised cheek. *Bastard! I'll make you pay for what you've done to me.*

He left the house, jumped in his car and drove into town, not even contemplating that Dawn's body was in the boot of his car. He left his vehicle in one of the multi-storey car parks and went in search of a phone shop.

"Hello, sir. How can I help?"

He pulled the collar of his jacket up around his face, trying to hide the bruises. "I need a pay-as-you-go phone. No damn contracts—thieving bastards, the lot of them."

"No problem, sir. You don't have to take out a contract if you don't want one. Would you like to come with me?"

He followed the young acne-covered man to the other side of the shop.

"What about this one? It's small yet high on functionality."

"Just the basic model, none of this fancy-pantsy stuff. All I want to do is make some calls in an emergency."

"Then this model would be ideal for you. It's one of our cheaper models, too, at only thirty-nine pounds."

"Sold. No need to bung it in a box, I'll have it as it is."

"Would you like me to set up the phone and register the sim card for you?"

"Yeah, that would be good. Thanks."

He stood tapping his foot impatiently while the young assistant did the necessary with the phone.

"There you are, it's all good to go now. Will it be cash or card, sir?"

"Cash." He handed over the forty pounds and waited for the phone and his change. Then he left the store swiftly and made his way back to the car, halting at the newsagent's when he remembered his promise to Geraldine. He nipped inside and bought five Sherbet Fountains, surprised they were still for sale after all these years.

He arrived home ten minutes later, eager to see Geraldine again. He took his bag upstairs and walked into the bedroom. She was lying down, her eyes wide open, staring at him. For the briefest of moments, he thought she was dead, but then she struggled to sit up. He let out a sigh of relief and dipped his hand inside the carrier and pulled out one of the Sherbet Fountains. He offered it to her.

Tentatively, Geraldine took the confectionery, but instead of ripping it open like his sister would have, she studied it, long and hard.

"Haven't you ever seen one before? Want me to show you how to eat it?"

He withdrew another fountain from the bag and sucked the end of the length of liquorice. His tongue tingled at the sensation of the sherbet filling his mouth. He cringed. It was far sweeter than he remembered. "Nice. Go on, try it."

Geraldine moved her other hand up to the one that was fastened to the bed and copied his movements exactly. As soon as the sherbet hit her mouth, she blinked, and her mouth twisted from side to side, as if she was unsure what to make of it. She threw the fountain on the floor.

He bent down to pick it up, unsure whether he should be offended or not, especially as he'd gone out of his way to pick up the confectionery for her. After a while he laughed. "Don't you like it? After tasting it, I'm inclined to agree with you. It's far too sweet for my liking. Never mind, at least I tried. Do you want something else to eat? A sandwich perhaps?" She shook her head. "You need to keep your strength up. Please, for me?"

She flopped down on the bed again and curled into a foetal position.

He left her and went downstairs. He threw the rest of the Sherbet Fountains in the bin and decided to switch on the news, mainly to see if his antics were the main topic on the bulletin. He wasn't disappointed.

He watched a female inspector speaking about the Flowers' deaths but thought it was strange that she made no reference to the last family he had slaughtered. He narrowed his eyes, focussing on the young inspector, annoyed that she didn't appear to be taking him seriously.

Suddenly, the filming was interrupted by another update. "That appeal was made earlier today. Since then, another heinous crime has taken place. It is with regret that I have to inform you that this morning Linda and Samuel Meredith were found murdered in their home. The attack was far more brutal than the first incident. This is Linda's sister, Katherine. Unfortunately, not only did the murderer kill two innocent people, he or she also appears to have kidnapped a third member of the family, the couple's daughter, Geraldine. Katherine would like to share with you all a little bit about her niece."

Katherine cleared her throat then took a sip of water from the glass by her side. "Thank you, Inspector." Holding up a framed photo, she added, "This is my beautiful family. My sister and her husband were kind, sincere and the most generous people I've ever met. They didn't deserve to die the way they did. To be cut down in the prime of their lives." She paused to wipe away the tears brimming in her eyes. "Their deaths will haunt me for the rest of my life, but my concerns lie with this young lady. My niece, Geraldine, has special needs. As you can probably tell from this picture, she has Down's syndrome. Up until now, Linda and Samuel ensured their daughter, my niece, led as normal a life as possible, but they were always there to guide her if she drifted off course. This morning, when the police arrived at my sister's home, Geraldine was missing. We're presuming that the murderer has kidnapped her. Unthinkable to even consider, but that appears to be the truth nonetheless. We need her back. Geraldine will be in a confused state without her parents being around her. If she witnessed their deaths, I dread to think how desperate she must be feeling right now. Please, I'm begging *you*, the person who is holding her, not to hurt her. She's the kindest, gentle soul. She doesn't deserve to be caught up in this."

Katherine reached for a small tube in front of her. Holding it up, she rattled it a little. "These are the tablets she needs to take daily. If she doesn't, you will have her death on your hands as well. Please, please let her go. Bring her home to me. She has a heart defect that needs to be carefully monitored at all times."

A lump formed in his throat when the woman broke down in tears. He had no idea that Geraldine needed constant supervision. All he'd seen when he'd spotted her in her bedroom was an older version of his sister. Something deep inside was urging him to care for her. Fraught, he ran his fingers through his hair. "What the fuck do I do now?"

He walked across the room and, still staring at the screen, he punched in the number running across the bottom.

"Hello, this is DS Jill Smalling. You're through to the incident room. How can I help?"

"I have her. The girl."

"Geraldine Meredith? Is that who you mean, sir?"

"You know damn well who I'm talking about. I want money for her safe return. Fifty grand."

"Would you hold the line, sir? I'll transfer your call to the SIO in charge of the case."

"Do that and I hang up. I want that money by tomorrow morning. I'll give you until midday to come up with the funds. It shouldn't be difficult, the aunt looks wealthy enough. If she wants her niece back as much as she's saying she does, then she'll be prepared to cough up the ransom, right?"

"I need some details from you, sir. Such as where you want us to drop off the funds."

He slammed a fist into his thigh. He should have thought about that. He'd placed the call without thinking through his plan thoroughly. "I'll be in touch tomorrow morning at ten with further instructions." He ended the call before the bitch copper could ask him anything else.

A heart defect! What if she goes downhill overnight without her medication? What the fuck am I going to do then?

He fixed himself a sandwich and a cup of coffee, but his throat was too restricted to eat. He pushed the sandwich aside. He tiptoed upstairs to check if Geraldine was all right. Glancing at her from the doorway, the way he used to watch Sonia sleep, he felt a peacefulness he hadn't felt in a long time. He wasn't a murderer, not really. He was a man who had been driven to extremes out of desperation to pay off the debts that had mounted up. Mick—it was Mick's fault! He was the one who had turned him into a killer. His greed to have his money returned plus an exorbitant percentage on top.

What the heck was I thinking taking the money off him in the first place? Drugs, the be all and end all of so many people's lives, that's my downfall. The one thing that is truly behind turning me into a killer. I never wanted this to happen. Never.

It was then that it dawned on him what he'd done. By making that call, was it possible the police could trace the call back to him? Yes, he'd bought a pay-as-you-go phone, but his dilemma remained the same: did he really know enough about the workings of the police's abilities to trace calls?

Scared, he picked up the phone and left the house. Pulling his hoodie over his head, he sprinted to his car and drove twenty minutes away to dump the phone. "Brilliant, now what do I do about getting the extra dosh I need to pay off Mick?" The answer came to him swiftly. He would need to find yet another victim, one with plenty of money lying around the house. He reached into the glove box and withdrew the Flowers' address book. Flicking through the pages, he chose his next victim. He started the engine and drove around the city for a couple of hours until darkness fell to shield his next movements.

He sat in the car and watched the house. The lights went on in different rooms periodically as the couple moved around inside. He clenched his hands tightly and unfurled his fingers as his nerves jangled. Although he'd carried out the same crime twice already, there was no denying how scared he was about taking someone else's life. If only the others had handed over the money, they would still be alive today. He wondered if this couple would be different or if they would be foolish enough to tackle him instead of handing over the cash he presumed they had in the house. He pulled the gaffer tape and the ten-inch knife from the carrier bag he kept under the passenger seat. He carefully slid the knife into the back of his jeans and placed the tape in the pocket of his jacket, then waited.

At ten-fifteen, he slipped out of the car, closing the door gently behind him. He crossed the road, surveying his surroundings every inch of the way until he reached the front door of the house. He peered through a gap at the side of the curtain and saw a man sitting in one of the easy chairs—he'd seen a light go on at the end of the house and presumed his wife had gone to bed. He knocked on the door, avoiding ringing the bell to alert the wife.

Not long after, the man opened the door. "Yes, can I help you?"

"Sorry. I appear to be lost. I saw your light on, I hope you don't mind me knocking."

"Not at all. Where are you looking for?"

"Bodenham. It's on this road somewhere, I know it is, just can't seem to place the right turning in the dark."

The man smiled and stepped towards him. "Is that your car?"

"It is."

"In that case, you'll need to turn the car around and go back to the end of the road. Drive for about two minutes, then you'll see a cross-roads. Take the first on your right."

"That's where I went wrong. Thanks ever so much." He withdrew the knife and pushed the man back into the house.

"What in God's name do you think you're doing?"

He struck the man with his clenched fist. The man toppled backwards, lost his balance and stared up at him from the floor. "Please, don't hurt us."

"I have no intention of hurting you if you hand over the money."

The man's brow creased into a frown. "What money? We don't keep any money in the house."

He leaned closer, getting in the man's face, and with a menacing sneer, he said, "I always kill the wife first, just so you know. She's in the bedroom, right? I might even have some fun with her before I kill her—that is unless you reconsider what you're telling me. Now, where do you keep the cash?"

The man sighed. "In the wardrobe, in a safe. Kill us, and you'll never get your hands on it. Let us live, and I'll give you the money and say nothing to the police."

"Are you bargaining with me?"

"All I'm trying to do is save our lives. Please, we don't want to die. We've only just retired. We have so many plans for the future—granted, those plans will go out the window once you take the money in the safe, but I'm willing to sacrifice our hard-earned cash in order to save our lives."

He threw the roll of tape at the man. "Tear a strip off and place it around your mouth and the back of your head."

"Please, there's no need for this. My wife and I are sensible people, we won't cause you any trouble, I promise you."

"That's as may be. Do it, now! I haven't got all night."

"Laurence? Is that you? Who are you speaking to?"

"It's all right, Tina. I just turned the TV up by mistake, love."

"Be more careful next time," his wife called back.

He wagged a finger at Laurence, mocking him. "Put the tape on."

Laurence unravelled a length of tape, ripped it off using his teeth and secured it around his mouth, overlapping it at the back of his head. The intruder forced the man to his feet, hooked an arm around his throat and held the blade to his cheek then pushed him towards the bedroom.

"Don't scream or I'll kill him," he ordered the woman who was sitting up in bed reading.

The woman's mouth dropped open, and she stared at her husband.

"I'm warning you, scream and it'll be the end for both of you. Tear off another length of tape," he instructed.

Laurence tore off a strip of tape. They walked towards the bed.

"Get out, nice and slowly. You try anything, and I'll slice his throat open."

"I won't, I swear. Please, I'm begging you, don't hurt us," the woman replied, her hands shaking when she pulled back the quilt and left the bed.

"Put it over her mouth." He kept the knife close to Laurence's cheek while he fastened the tape around his wife's mouth.

With the couple's mouths secured, he thrust the man away from him. The husband and wife clenched each other's hands tightly and stared at him.

"Do as I say, and I promise I won't hurt you. Where's the safe?"

The man turned to look over his shoulder and pointed at the louvered wardrobes along one of the walls.

He jabbed the knife, urging the man to move. "Show me."

Laurence left his wife and crossed the room to the wardrobe. The intruder motioned for the wife to go with her husband and then followed the couple. Laurence opened the wardrobe door and swept the clothes to one end of the rail. He stood back and pointed at the small safe lying at the back of the wardrobe.

"Don't just stand there, open it."

Laurence got down on his knees, wincing as he lowered himself, his bones cracking, objecting to the position he was getting himself into. He fiddled with the dial on the safe, back and forth until the door clicked open.

"Get the money out and put it on the floor."

Laurence withdrew two large bundles of money. He ducked down to see if there was anything left in the safe—there was, another bundle of money.

The intruder pointed the knife at the wife. "All of it. Don't mess with me or I will kill her, just like I killed your friends."

Laurence dove back into the safe and extracted the other bundle. He threw it on the floor with the other two and looked up at him.

He pulled a carrier bag from his pocket and gave it to Laurence. "Put the money in there, quickly."

Once Laurence had filled the bag, he held it up for him to take.

Now what do I do with them? They've seen my face. In spite of the promises I made to them, how can I let them go? His inner voices argued with each other whether he should leave the couple alive or kill them. But the decision was taken out of his hands when the wife surprised him by smashing a large ornament over his head. He automatically struck out with the knife, catching the woman in her abdomen. She doubled over as blood instantly soaked her nightdress. Her legs gave way beneath her, and she tumbled to the floor. Laurence cried out, the sound muffled by the tape on his mouth. He rushed to be with his wife.

"I warned her what would happen. I had no intention of hurting either of you. Now I'm going to be forced to kill you both."

Laurence glanced up, his eyes pleading with him not to carry out his threat.

He was in two minds what to do next. The woman had forced his hand by attacking him. He had to punish her. Regret filtered through him. He was also conscious of how long he'd left Geraldine by herself. He was now anxious to get back to see how she was.

He stabbed the wife repeatedly, her husband trying to shield the blows but not getting very far due to his sobbing. Then he turned his knife on the husband, thrusting the blade over and over into the man's chest and stomach until both of them lay motionless on the floor at his feet.

He searched the bedside tables and the bottom of the other wardrobe and withdrew the personal file the couple kept there. Moments later, he ran from the house, leaving the door wide open in his haste. He threw the bag and the file onto the back seat of the car and started the engine. He roared away from the house and drove all the way home as if he was guiding the car on autopilot. His mind replayed the evening's events, pondering where it had all gone wrong. It should have been an easy task: rob the couple of their money and flee the property. The woman's foolish actions had changed all that in a heartbeat.

No one tries to pull a fast one on me.

There was one compensation for the couple's murder. This time he had secured enough cash to pay off his debts. He sighed, relieved he'd finally paid Mick off—at least he would do come Friday morning. He'd think about the consequences once he was debt free.

He pulled the car into a space outside the house he rented. Picking up the carrier bag and file, he entered the house and hid them along with the other money in the cupboard under the stairs. Going to the fridge, he removed a bottle of beer and flicked off the top. He downed half the contents of the cold liquid in a matter of seconds. With the bottle in his hand, he crept up the stairs to check on Geraldine. He peered into the bedroom to find her in the same position he'd left her in. She was snoring gently. He smiled and closed the door, then went back downstairs and flopped onto the couch. He removed his bloody trousers and swiftly fell asleep, exhausted by his day's exploits.

CHAPTER 13

Sara had been full of recriminations since she'd missed the call from the killer. Why hadn't she answered the phone to him? If she had, she might have been able to bargain with him to let Geraldine go. Now, with the deadline looming the following day of when he was going to make further contact, Sara had a feeling that yet again, sleep was about to evade her that night. She'd not long slipped into bed when her mobile rang. Switching on the light, she answered it. "Hello."

"Sorry to disturb at this late hour, ma'am. I have a note on the system that you should be contacted immediately should something like this happen, no matter what time of the day it is."

She groaned inwardly, fearing what she was about to be told, and threw back the quilt. "Go on. I'm listening. What have you got?"

"Looks like another murder out in the sticks, ma'am. Well, one murder and another severely injured victim."

"He left one alive? Male or female? Where?" She fired off the questions and put the phone on speaker while she tore off her pyjamas and stepped into the clothes she'd worn that day over clean underwear she'd taken from her chest of drawers.

"Male. The husband, ma'am. He's been rushed to A&E. The couple live out at Felton."

"Crap, similar sort of area, am I right?"

"Yes, ma'am. Within a five-mile radius of the other victims. Can I take it you'll be attending, ma'am?"

"Of course. I'm getting dressed now. Do me a favour and give Carla Jameson a ring for me. Ask her to meet me at the address, which is what, by the way?"

"Will do, ma'am. Number six Grasmere Lane, Felton."

"Thanks. I'm on my way. ETA fifteen minutes at the most."

"Very well, ma'am. Thank you."

Sara finished dressing, kissed a sleepy Misty on the top of her head and dashed down the stairs. She picked up her handbag, checked her pocket for her ID and left the house.

Her mobile rang as she left her village. "Carla, sorry about this. Are you okay to attend?"

"Yep. Getting dressed now. I should be with you in thirty minutes, boss."

"No rush. Drive safely."

"You too."

Sara entered the road to find it lit up with various response vehicles, and the pathologist's van was already at the scene. Before approaching the house, she slipped on a paper suit and protective shoes. *Here I go again!*

She made her way up the path and almost bumped into Lorraine who was leaving the house. "Whoa! Nearly. What's the rush?"

"I was in such a hurry to get in the house I forgot my bag. Unlucky us, both being called out at this time of night, right?"

"You could say that. Is it bad?"

Lorraine swept past her. "It's never good when murder is involved, Inspector," she said tersely.

Sara felt ashamed for her choice of wording. She waited for Lorraine to return before venturing inside the house. "Sorry."

Lorraine frowned and eased past her again. "For what?"

"What I said. I was told there's one casualty and one deceased."

"Shall we go inside or carry on this conversation out here?"

They entered the house together.

"Is the crime scene in the bedroom again?"

"It is. Bloody mess. At first glance, there's a safe in the wardrobe. That is now open and empty. I guess that's your motive."

"All this is about money? This person is either desperate or has racked up a lot of debt he needs to pay off."

"That's my take on it. We need to catch this bastard, and quickly."

Sara shrugged. "I'm trying. But with no DNA or evidence to go on it's proving mighty difficult. We have to catch a break soon, right?"

"Maybe the husband will turn out to be a good witness, if he pulls through. He was pretty cut up himself. His wife was possibly stabbed ten to fifteen times. I'll know more when I open her up. Shocking all the same. We need to put a halt to this, Sara."

Sara shrugged, a feeling of hopelessness descending.

"Hi, I'm here." Carla shouted from the door.

"Have you got a suit in your car?" Sara asked.

"No. I've run out."

"Grab one from my van," Lorraine instructed.

Carla left the doorway and reappeared a few minutes later, dressed appropriately for the occasion.

"Okay, can we go through to the bedroom now?" Sara asked, eager to get on.

The three of them walked up the hallway and into the main bedroom. The deceased woman was lying on the floor at the foot of the bed, her body twisted. The cream-coloured carpet directly beneath her bed was now a dark maroon.

"Damn. Why? Crap, why kill them?" Sara scratched her neck.

"Exactly. If this is about the money, then why not take it and run? Why go to the extreme of killing them?" Lorraine asked, frustration evident in her tone.

"And why haven't we found Geraldine yet, either dead or alive?" Carla added.

"Good point. One that has been puzzling me all day," Sara admitted, glancing around. She crossed the room to another patch of blood in the carpet. "I take it this is where the husband was found?"

Lorraine nodded. "Correct."

"Do we know what his chances are?"

"Not at this stage. You'll need to contact the hospital."

Sara moved towards the wardrobe and crouched. "I wonder if it was worth it. How much money was in the safe? We need to find a relative, see if they can fill us in. Carla, get on to the station, see if we can get the ball rolling on that at least."

"Will do." Carla withdrew her phone from her pocket and tutted. "I'm going to have to go outside, no reception in here."

Sara walked around the room, observing the victim's body from different angles, hoping that something useful would stand out to help them begin their investigation. But there was nothing. She growled in frustration. "What is this guy's problem to rob these people of their lives just at the age they should be enjoying themselves? Why target pensioners? It can't only be about the money, can it?"

"I really can't answer that except to say that people of this generation aren't likely to be riddled with debt and generally have money lying around because of their lack of trust with banks, as with the Flowers. Heartbreaking all the same."

"I'm wondering if they're all connected. I need to delve more into that side of things in the morning. If they are, then how does the killer know them all? Has he worked for them?"

"A tradesman? You might be onto something there. Good luck finding out that information. Right, I'm going to have to get on. I'm keen to be out of here by midnight if at all possible. I have a PM booked in for nine in the morning. I'd like to get some shuteye before then if I can."

"Of course. Just ignore me. One last thing...who found the couple?"

"The neighbour said he saw the front door wide open when he was putting some rubbish in his bin. He came over to investigate and called it in."

"Thanks. I'll drop by and see him before we leave." Sara left the bedroom and walked back through the house and into the lounge. Carla joined her a few seconds later. "Any good?"

Carla nodded. "Yes. The couple have a daughter called Jenny, living in Hereford. I've got her number and address."

"Good. I really don't want to do this over the phone. We'll take a ride over there."

"Want me to follow you?"

"Might as well. Let's get this out of the way and call it a day. I think we're going to have a heck of a day ahead of us tomorrow."

"You're not wrong there. The desk sergeant just informed me that the phones have been busy this evening, since the appeal went out."

Sara exhaled and puffed out her cheeks. "I wonder if the killer has made contact again. Either way, I sense we're going to be over-whelmed with information soon on this one. I hope that's the case anyway. Let's go. I'll nip and see the neighbour first, tell him that one of the team will be out here first thing in the morning to take down a statement."

Sara had a brief chat with the neighbour who said he saw no one hanging around the house at all. She arranged a rendezvous time the following day to take his statement and bid the gentleman farewell.

CHAPTER 14

The detached house in Huntington was in darkness when they arrived—not surprising, considering it was almost eleven-thirty.

Sara rang the bell. She and Carla waited patiently. A light in the bedroom above turned on, and a woman peered out of the window at them. She opened the door a few seconds later, pulling her dressing gown tight around her middle.

Sara flashed her warrant card. "Hello, are you Jenny? I'm DI Sara Ramsey, and this is my partner, Carla Jameson."

"I am. What on earth is this about? How dare you come to the door at this time of night? What's the meaning of this intrusion?"

Sara smiled. "It would be better if we spoke inside, Jenny."

She nodded, let them in and led them through to the rear of the house to the large kitchen.

Sara headed towards the round glass table and pulled out a chair. "Take a seat, Jenny."

The woman appeared stunned as if she knew what was coming next. She sat in the chair and waited until Sara and Carla had each taken a seat, then asked, "What's this about? Please, don't tell me this has anything to do with my parents."

Sara swallowed and nodded. "I'm sorry to have to inform you that your parents were both attacked in their home this evening."

Jenny buried her head in her hands. "No. There must be some mistake. I only spoke to Mum earlier on."

"What time was that?"

"Around nine." Jenny dropped her hands and asked, "Are they both dead?"

"Sorry, your mother passed away at the scene, but your father survived the attack and is in hospital."

Jenny pushed back her chair and stood. "I need to get dressed. I should be with him." She tried to turn, but her legs appeared weak and failed to work.

"Take it easy, Jenny. Let the news sink in first. There's no rush."

Jenny flopped back into her chair and sobbed. She kept repeating 'how unfair life is' under her breath. "They were going abroad next week, hoping to buy a holiday home with their savings."

Sara and Carla exchanged glances.

How much money was there in that safe? "Is it possible for you to tell us how much money they had?"

"Not much really. Enough to buy them a small apartment in Spain. Around forty thousand pounds. They kept it in a safe in the bedroom. No, please don't tell me that someone has taken that money."

Sara sighed. "That's exactly what they've done. Your father must have put up a fight; he's still fighting now."

"But he wasn't able to save my beautiful mother."

"No, no one was able to save her. I'm afraid she died at the scene before the ambulance arrived."

Jenny wiped her eyes on the sleeve of her velour dressing gown. "I should get dressed and ring a taxi. I don't trust myself to get there in one piece if I drive."

"There's no need. I can take you to the hospital when you're ready to leave. Can I make you a drink of tea or coffee?" Sara suggested.

"A cup of tea might help. I'll be fine. I think I can make it upstairs without my legs giving way this time. I won't be long."

Sara busied herself with making a drink for all of them while Carla contacted the A&E department to see if there was any news on Jenny's father. He was in surgery; they were trying to repair a puncture to his lungs.

"Let's not tell her that just yet," Sara whispered once Carla shared the news.

When Jenny came back into the room, her eyes were red and swimming with fresh tears. She wore a pair of jeans and a large thick jumper. Sara placed a mug of tea on the table along with the sugar canister. "I haven't sugared it."

"I don't usually have it, but I think I'm in need of a sugar rush. Have you heard how Dad is?"

"Not yet. We'll soon find out."

While they drank, Jenny sighed periodically for the loss of her mother. Sara patted her hand to comfort her.

Ten minutes later, they left the house. Sara instructed Carla to go home—there was no point both of them going to hospital to sit with Jenny. "I'll see you in the morning."

S ara parked the car, and together, she and Jenny rushed into the busy A&E department. Sara flashed her ID. "DI Sara Ramsey. A Mr Haldon was brought in a few hours ago. Can you tell us what's going on please?"

"If you'd like to take a seat in the family room, I'll get a doctor to come and see you."

"Thanks." Sara led Jenny through the corridor to the family room a few yards away. They sat in silence and waited for the doctor to appear. Half an hour later, a petite female doctor joined them.

"Hi, I'm Doctor Jones."

"Hello, Doctor. I'm DI Sara Ramsey. This is Mr Haldon's daughter, Jenny. How is he?"

The doctor smiled briefly. "He's alive. That's all we can say at this point. He's gone down to surgery to repair a tear in his lung. We're hopeful that nothing will go wrong while he's under anaesthetic, but I have to tell you he's a long way off being out of the woods yet. It really depends on how strong he is physically as to whether he pulls through this."

Jenny sniffled. "He's a fighter, though whether he'll continue to fight when he finds out about Mum is another matter entirely. When can I see him?"

"Not for a good few hours yet. The surgery could take anything between an hour and four, depending on the severity of the hole they need to plug. I'm sorry I can't give you more than that. You're welcome to wait here for him, and we'll come and fetch you when he's in recovery."

"Thank you, we appreciate that, Doctor," Sara replied, throwing an arm around Jenny to support her in case her legs gave way again.

"My pleasure." The doctor left the room.

Sara guided Jenny to a seat. "Can I get you anything?"

"Apart from the obvious, like bringing my mother back to life and ensuring my father gets through his surgery okay? No, thank you. Sorry for snapping, this is very hard for me to handle. We lost my brother in a car accident only last year. Mum has had a problematic year dealing with her grief, and now this…"

"I'm sorry. I had no idea."

"Look, I'll be fine. There's really no point in you staying here with me."

"I'd like to, just for a few hours at least." Sara was dying to curl up in her own bed, but the thought of leaving the woman alone to deal with such a fraught situation didn't sit well with her in the slightest.

"If you insist. I really need you to be out there trying to find the maniac who carried out this awful crime. My parents didn't deserve this. No one deserves to go through this. I saw you on the news earlier —sorry, that has only just hit me. Do you think those cases are connected to what went on at my parents' house?"

"I'm inclined to think that way, yes. The last thing I want to do is start bombarding you with questions right now, but I do have one I'd like to ask, if that's okay?"

Jenny nodded. "If I can answer it, I will."

"Do you know if your parents knew Ted and Maureen Flowers?"

Jenny frowned. "Gosh, the name rings a bell at the back of my mind, so I'm going to say yes. They're the couple who were killed earlier this week, right?"

"Unfortunately, yes. What about Linda and Samuel Meredith?"

"Again, I think so."

"That's what I suspected. The person responsible for all the crimes that have taken place this week knew each of the couples."

"How? Can you give me more to go on than that?"

Sara shrugged. "Not at this time. Maybe they've employed the person recently to do some kind of work to their homes. We're really unsure at present. Do you recall your parents having any form of contractor in their home in the last few weeks?"

"No, nothing along those lines. Dad is really handy around the house. He would have to be out of his depth to call a proper tradesman in."

"And are you in regular contact with your parents?"

"Yes, we ring each other all the time. They would have told me if anything like that had happened."

"Hopefully, the calls we've received from the appeal being aired tonight will give us a better idea of what we're dealing with. If there's a killer on the loose in Hereford, then someone knows who that killer is."

"Wait, what about the woman who has been abducted? Surely someone will come forward if they witness her in distress with this person, or am I being foolish to think people care enough nowadays?"

"It's a consideration. That was our intention in showing a picture of Geraldine, in the hope it will trigger something in someone's mind. The killer has to be living locally. He seems to know the area where your parents live like the back of his hand."

"I hope something comes to light for you soon. I'd hate for yet another family to have to go through what I'm going through right now."

"We're going to try our best to ensure that doesn't happen." Sara hoped her words didn't sound hollow. She was desperate to find the culprit herself.

CHAPTER 15

It was gone three in the morning when Sara finally slipped her key into the front door of her home. Misty was there to welcome her in spite of the late hour. She swept her cat into her arms and buried her head in her fur. Misty purred contentedly. "Come on, you, back to bed. I hope I can bloody sleep. I better set my alarm ten minutes earlier just in case I have trouble opening my eyes later."

Sara undressed and crawled into bed. She drifted off to sleep, but her recurring nightmare woke her only an hour later. She was drenched in sweat. She kicked off the quilt, forgetting that Misty was curled up on the bed beside her. After splashing cold water on her face, she dried herself and returned to her bed.

Her attempt to get further sleep proved futile. In the end, she got up at six and fixed herself a fry-up to set her up for the long day she suspected lay ahead of her.

After showering and sorting through her wardrobe for a comfortable suit to wear, she left the house and drove into work.

For the third morning on the trot, Carla was already at her desk when Sara arrived. "Crikey, there was me feeling pleased as Punch about probably beating you into work this morning. Couldn't you sleep?"

"Nope. Could you?"

Sara shook her head. "I think I managed an hour or so. I didn't get home until three. Is there something concerning you that you'd like to share with me?"

Carla tilted her head. "Honestly, no, there's nothing. I can't sleep when Andrew is away. He should be back either today or tomorrow."

"Ah, ain't that sweet. It must be love," Sara ribbed her partner.

"Whatever. I'm not the hearts-and-roses type, but there's something about having a man to share your bed…shit! I'm sorry. Me and my big mouth."

"No need to apologise. I'm happy that you have someone to share your life with. Hang on to him, treat him well, because you never know what's around the corner. Bugger, listen to me. Ignore me being maudlin at this time of the day. Coffee?"

"Please."

Sara bought two white coffees from the machine and returned to Carla's desk. "Why the sad face?"

"No reason. Hate suffering from foot-in-mouth disease, that's all."

Sara walked towards her office and called out, "I'm not listening. It's forgotten about already. Let me see what joys the postman has brought while I down my coffee, and I'll be with you soon. We've got a lot to get through today."

She paused at the window to see the sun rising over the Brecon Beacons in the distance and sighed. Such a beautiful place. Why on earth would someone bring all the darkness to its door? She continued to her desk, ripped open the post and sorted it into the relevant piles of urgency. Then, coffee in hand, she returned to the incident room to find all the team sitting at their desks.

Carla smiled. "I rang them and asked them to come in early."

A warm glow swept through Sara. She was proud to have such an amazing group of people working under her. "I appreciate it, guys. Do you want to gather around?"

Everyone turned their chair to face her.

Sara sighed when she glanced at the two whiteboards sitting side by side. "Bugger, we're going to need another one of these. Never mind, we'll sort that out later. Talking to the last victims' daughter at the hospital in the early hours of this morning, we came to the conclusion that there is possibly a connection between all three families. That's where our priorities lie today, finding what type of connection that is. Barry, why don't you and Jill do that? Our other main focus needs to be to go through the calls we've received overnight from the appeal. Christine and Scott, why don't you sift through those, see what shows up? Will and Marissa, I'd like you to go out to the Haldons' home and question the neighbours. One of them reported seeing the front door open—he's the one who rang 999. I need you to take his statement and interview the other neighbours, see if they possibly saw anyone hanging around. Jenny said she spoke to her mother on the phone at nine. I received the call to go to the property around ten-thirty, I believe it was. Check with control what time the 999 call came in—that should give you a timeline to work to. Okay, let's get to it, guys."

The team dispersed. Carla glanced at her and shrugged. "What do you want me to do?"

Sara tutted. "We need to stick around in case the killer tries to make contact again. He mentioned calling back at ten with instructions. My thoughts are that he won't bother doing that now."

"May I ask why?"

"Intuition is telling me that he received a large haul from his last job, somewhere around forty grand, Jenny said. Therefore, I'd like us to concentrate our efforts on trying to locate Geraldine. Why don't you ring the desk sergeant? He was sending a search party out to the Merediths' house yesterday. See if anything came of it. I doubt it, otherwise we would have heard. It doesn't hurt to chase things up, though."

"On it."

"While you're at it, ask him to send up another whiteboard for the third victim. I'm going to ring the hospital, see if there's any news regarding Laurence Haldon." She rushed into her office to make the call.

After being patched through to the intensive care unit, the duty sister on the ward told her that Jenny was still sitting by her father's bedside. The operation had been a success, but they were still waiting for him to regain consciousness. Sara hung up and sat back in her chair, willing Laurence Haldon to come round and tell them who the culprit was.

CHAPTER 16

He crept around the house. It was seven-thirty. Geraldine had been asleep all night, and he was trying his hardest not to wake her. He poked his head into the room and heard something that didn't sit right with him. Memories of what his sister had gone through flooded his mind. He walked towards the bed and peered at Geraldine. Her eyes were puffy. His nostrils twitched at the smell when he got closer to the bed. She'd wet herself.

No shit, Sherlock. How the hell was she supposed to get to the toilet when I've tied her to the bed?

He bashed his clenched fists on either side of his head. He was panicking now, aware that she wasn't well. "Geraldine, can you hear me, sweetheart?"

She didn't respond.

He paced the room, tearing his hair from its roots. "Damn, now what am I going to do? I can't leave her like this, she needs her medication. I need to get her to the hospital."

He untied her wrist. Ignoring the smell, he hoisted her onto his shoulder and carried her down the stairs. She was heavier than he'd predicted she would be. Once he'd reached the front door, he propped her up against the wall and opened the door. After checking the coast was clear, he hoisted her back onto his shoulder again, took out his keys to the car, pressed the key fob and ran up the path before anyone could spot him. He opened the car door and gently placed Geraldine in the back seat.

The hospital was at least ten minutes away. The traffic was flowing well—none of the usual snarl-ups at that time of the morning, much to his relief. He pulled his hood up, ready to dive into A&E. Two minutes later, he left the car running, dashed into the hospital and emerged with a wheelchair he'd found lying around in the hallway. He placed Geraldine in the chair, kissed her cheek lightly and wheeled her into the A&E department. With his head down, he rushed up to the reception desk. "She needs help. I have to go."

"Stop! Sir, you can't just dump her here. Wait!"

"She needs medication. I'm outta here."

"Stop! Somebody stop him. Don't let him leave," the receptionist frantically cried out.

Luckily for him, there were no security guards or other nursing staff around. He escaped with ease and ran back to his car. His emotions were all over the place. Predominantly, he feared that he'd endangered Geraldine's life unnecessarily by abducting her. "Pull through, little lady. I never meant to harm you. I never meant to harm anyone. All I ever wanted was the cash."

CHAPTER 17

Sara was sitting in her office with Carla going over possible scenarios on what they should do next regarding Geraldine's safe return when the call came in.

"Ma'am, it's Jeff on the front desk."

"Hi, Jeff. What's up?"

"I think I have some good news for you. I've had a call from the hospital."

"I'm listening. What are you getting so excited about, Jeff?" Sara gestured with her hand as if to urge the desk sergeant to hurry up.

Carla chuckled.

"Sorry, ma'am, I'm a tad emotional. She's there, at the hospital."

"You're not making sense. Who are you talking about? Jenny Haldon?"

The desk sergeant took a deep breath then said, "No, ma'am, Geraldine. He's only gone and taken her to the hospital."

"Jesus! Really? That's excellent news. Wait, is she okay?" She held her thumb up to Carla and smiled cautiously.

"They think she's going to be okay, ma'am. She was in dire need of her medication. But he did the right thing taking her there rather than dumping her on the street."

"I agree. Thanks for letting me know. I'll ring her aunt and share the good news."

"You're welcome, ma'am."

Sara hung up and punched her fist in the air. "We've got her. Let me ring Katherine."

Carla smiled and left her seat. "I'll tell the others."

"Katherine, it's Sara Ramsey. Are you sitting down?"

"Oh no, that sounds ominous. Yes, I'm sitting in the garden doing my crossword, trying to keep my mind occupied."

"Can you join me at the hospital?"

"What? Why?"

"Because Geraldine has just shown up there. I don't know any more than that at this stage."

"Oh heavens! Is she all right? Please don't tell me the bastard has hurt her."

"As far as I know, he hasn't hurt her. Can you make your own way there or do you want me to pick you up?"

"No. I can get there under my own steam, I think."

"Okay, drive carefully. I'll meet you in the Accident and Emergency Department soon. This is good news, Katherine."

"I might not sound excited, but I'm thrilled, I promise."

"See you soon."

"Thank you, Sara."

She ended the call and let out a relieved sigh that ended with a huge smile.

She's safe. Thank God for that! He hadn't done the unthinkable to her. But why? Why has he let her go? Because he didn't want her death on his hands? How bad is she? There's only one way to find out.

She jumped out of her chair and entered the incident room, tugging on her jacket while she walked. "I'm going to the hospital. Katherine is joining me there. Carla, why don't you stay here to ensure all the angles are covered and collate any information that comes in?"

"Fine by me, boss. Excellent news that Geraldine is safe. Do we know if she's okay? He hasn't hurt her, has he?"

"I'm getting the impression he hasn't. I'll know more when I get there. I'll see you later."

Sara arrived at the hospital and spotted Katherine pulling into the car park close to the main entrance. She waited for her to join her.

Katherine smiled and hugged her. "Thank you for all you've done."

"I really didn't do anything. I've had time to think on the drive over here. My take is that you making the appeal did the trick. If the person who had her saw that, maybe your plea touched a nerve and pricked their conscience."

"You really think so? I've often watched the police appeals on TV and wondered if they truly made any difference. I guess they do if she's back with us. I'm dying to see her. It's going to be a bittersweet moment. We don't know yet if she's aware of what has happened to Linda and Samuel."

Sara linked arms with Katherine and steered her towards the entrance. "We're about to find out."

A&E was surprisingly busy when they walked into the reception area.

"Can I help you?" asked the brunette young woman with rosy cheeks sitting at the desk.

Sara flashed her ID. "I received a call to say Geraldine Meredith was here. This is her aunt. Would it be possible for us to see her?"

"If you'd like to wait here a moment, I'll get someone to come and have a chat with you."

"Thanks." Sara and Katherine stepped away from the desk and the small queue behind them and waited anxiously for the woman to return. "Here she is now."

The receptionist was accompanied by a tall male dressed in a light-blue uniform. "Hi, if you'd like to come with me, I'll take you to see Geraldine now."

"How is she?" Katherine asked.

"She's doing better now. We've given her some of her medication, and she's improving bit by bit."

"Did he hurt her? The person who abducted her?" Sara asked.

"I don't think so. It's hard to tell. She hasn't spoken at all, and we didn't want to put her through the ordeal of bombarding her with questions. You might consider that when you see her."

Sara raised her hands. "Don't worry. I'll give her the time she needs to recover."

The nurse smiled. "She's going to need it."

"Is she aware of anything?" Katherine asked.

"Not really. She's a little bewildered, but I'm sure she'll be fine soon."

Katherine tutted. "I doubt she'll ever be the same again if she saw her parents slaughtered."

"Let's hope she didn't see that, Katherine. The truth is, we don't know if she's even aware of their deaths," Sara stated.

He led them the short distance to the cubicles and swept the curtain back a little to allow them access to one on the right. Geraldine was sitting up in bed, cuddling a bright-pink teddy bear.

"Geraldine, my darling. How are you?" Katherine rushed forward to hug her niece.

Geraldine seemed panicked by the gesture, her eyes wide as saucers. She turned her head to the side and receded back into the pillow propping her up when Katherine tried to kiss her cheek.

Glancing over at Sara, Katherine looked hurt. Sara gave her a reassuring smile, pleading for her to be patient with her niece after going through such a traumatic ordeal.

Sara gestured for Katherine to sit beside Geraldine. Once seated, Katherine reached out a hand for her niece to hold, but Geraldine clung to the teddy bear and ignored her aunt's affections.

"Hello, Geraldine. My name is Sara Ramsey. How are you feeling?"

Geraldine stared at her, her eyes increasing and decreasing in size at regular intervals as if wondering if she could trust Sara. Then she buried her head in the teddy bear.

"Give her time," the nurse said. "I'll be back in a while."

He slipped through the curtain. Geraldine's chest inflated and deflated rapidly in an instant. Sara smiled, trying to reassure the young woman that she was now safe and out of imminent danger.

"Did he hurt you?" Katherine whispered.

Geraldine hugged the bear tighter. Small tears dripped onto her cheeks. Finally, Geraldine found her voice. "He hurt Mummy and Daddy."

"I know, sweetheart," Katherine said, her voice catching in her throat.

"But did he hurt you, Geraldine?" Sara asked quietly.

"No. He was nice to me. That was until he gave me that awful stuff that exploded in my mouth." Geraldine shuddered and groaned a little.

Katherine and Sara exchanged puzzled glances. *What could that have been? Exploded in her mouth?* Sara was at a loss to know what she meant. Did he try to force her to take the wrong type of medication perhaps? Or do drugs?

Her aunt squeezed her hand. "Never mind, love. He did the right thing and brought you to hospital."

Sara smiled. "Did he tell you his name, Geraldine?"

She vehemently shook her head, dashing any hopes that Sara had of possibly identifying the man during her visit. She decided not to push it further.

Sara remained at the hospital for another hour while Geraldine struggled to keep her eyes open and spoke to her aunt. She then rushed back to the station, delighted that Geraldine was safe, frustrated, however, that she wasn't able to pass on any useful clues that would help apprehend the killer swiftly. It would be down to old-fashioned police work in that case, unless Laurence Haldon regained consciousness soon.

CHAPTER 18

"**S**he's fine," Sara announced to the team the second she entered the incident room.

Everyone seemed relieved to hear the news.

"That's a relief," Carla said, jumping out of her seat to buy Sara a coffee.

"Geraldine's shaken up a little. She was able to tell us that the man hurt her parents but he was nice to her. She also said that he gave her something that exploded in her mouth. Anyone know what that likely was? Are there any drugs on the market that will do that?"

The team all appeared perplexed by the question.

"Nothing is coming to mind," Carla admitted. "Want me to get on to the drug squad, see if they can think of anything?"

Sara nodded. "Excellent idea. I think he saw the appeal, heard that she needed medication and tried to possibly supplement her normal drugs. Maybe if we can find out what he gave her, we'll be able to trace it back to a supplier. Or is that just me being optimistic?"

Carla shrugged. "It's sure worth a shot." She picked up her phone and dialled a number.

Sara drifted into her office, pausing at the window to take a sip from her coffee. She needed to gather her thoughts and decide in which direction the case should go next. She had hoped the phones would be ringing off the hook by now—clearly that wasn't the case. After the initial flurry of calls, things had died down considerably. Unfortunately for them.

Carla knocked on the door and joined her a few minutes later. "Sorry, they didn't have a clue, boss. In fact, they said that was a new one on them and something they'd need to be aware of going forward. They thanked us for the heads-up, cheeky buggers."

"Oh well, it was worth a shot. What are we missing on this case, Carla? I have a feeling deep in my gut that it's something obvious, and yet I can't put my finger on it."

"I haven't got a clue, if I'm honest. What do you want to do now?"

"Let me finish my coffee, and we'll go over what has been learnt this morning with the team. Everyone is back now, yes?"

"They are. I'll leave you in peace for a moment then. Are you sure you're okay?"

"Yep, I'm fine. Just frustrated, that's all. I'm not sure what lies ahead for Geraldine now."

"Won't Katherine give her a home?"

"I'm not sure. I'd like to think so; however, if I put myself in Katherine's shoes, would I be willing to give up my freedom to become Geraldine's constant carer?"

"It's a tough dilemma to be confronted with. I suppose blood is thicker than water in this instance, right?"

"You'd like to think so. Katherine seems a genuinely nice person, but who can tell what lies ahead of them? I'll be out shortly."

Carla left the room. Sara sat behind her desk to finish her drink while she dealt with another batch of post that had magically appeared on her desk, adding to her frustration. Opening the first letter, she let out a long sigh. Yet another change in procedure she needed to instruct her team about.

Why don't they leave well alone and let us get on with policing the damn county, or is that too much to ask?

Her mobile tinkled, indicating that someone had left her a voicemail.

"Hi, it's me, Donald. Long time no hear...sorry, I appreciate how busy you are working the case. Felt proud when I saw you on TV yesterday. No pressure from me, just wanted to warn you that Mum mentioned she was going to be getting in touch with you soon. Fore-warned and all that. Speak soon. Thinking of you always. Bye."

Sara leaned her head back against the headrest and groaned. "Jesus, that's all I need to have, Charlotte bending my ear about why I haven't been over to see them in months."

"Sorry, did you say something?" Carla asked, appearing in the doorway.

"Nope. Only sitting here having a conversation with myself. That's normal, right?"

Carla shook her head. "Not really. I'm willing to make an exception in your case. I have some news that might be of interest to you."

Tossing her mobile on the desk, Sara sat upright in her chair. "Go on."

"A call has come in regarding the appeal."

"A call? Has the killer rung back?"

"Nope, try again."

"Has someone offered up a name possibly?" Sara's heart rate increased in tempo.

"You've got it in one—well, at the second attempt."

"And? Don't keep a girl waiting."

"Why don't I tell you on the way? The caller said the person of interest is at his establishment now."

"Crap! What are we waiting for?"

They rushed out of the office and down the stairs, almost bumping into the DCI at the bottom. "Hey, what's the hurry?" she asked.

"Sorry, boss. Need to fly. Can I touch base with you when I return?"

"I'll be expecting you. You and I have a lot to discuss, Inspector."

"Be back soon, ma'am," Sara shouted, bolting out the front door. "Damn, that sounds bloody worrying. She's probably annoyed that I haven't been in touch to keep her up to date. How can I when we have nothing to go on?"

"Hopefully, that will all change in half an hour or so."

"You said it. Where are we going?"

"The Red Lion, out near Rotherwas. I'll give you the directions."

"You'll need to, I've never heard of it." Once they were en route, Sara said, "Spill the beans."

"The landlord said that one of his customers has been coming into the bar most of the week with what appears to be blood on his trainers. It wasn't until he saw the appeal go out that he thought it best to ring us. The guy just walked in."

"Interesting. Well, we do have a bloody footprint that we need a match for. Let's hope this turns out to be the break we need—we could sure do with one."

"Fingers crossed."

The pub was situated fifteen minutes away from the station. When they arrived, there were six or seven vehicles in the car park.

"Good, it doesn't look too busy. I hope he doesn't cause a scene," Sara said.

"I hope so, too. Maybe one of the boys should have come with us just in case."

"Too late now. We'll handle him."

They entered the public bar and approached the barman serving behind the counter. "Are you the manager?"

The man leaned in. "Yes. Are you the police?"

"We are. I won't bother showing my ID in case it causes a disturbance. Where is he?"

"At the pool table in the next room. I've been keeping an eye on him. He's the one with longish black hair. Andy Somers is his name."

"Thanks. Leave it with us. We appreciate you getting in touch."

"I've got a cricket bat if you need it."

Sara smiled. "I'm sure we'll be fine. Most offenders don't like to make a scene in public."

"It's here if you change your mind."

Sara and Carla left the lounge bar and walked through the door on the right to the public bar. The pool table was the central attraction in the room. Two men were playing a game while another three watched.

"Are you ready for this?" Sara asked out the corner of her mouth.

"Yep. I've got my fingers ready to jab in his eyes if the need arises."

Sara chuckled and strode towards the table with Carla a few feet behind her. "Hi, gents, I'm looking for Andy Somers."

Four of the men turned to face Somers, but he was bent over the table about to take a shot. He stood upright and placed his cue in front of him, gripping it with one hand above the other. "That's me. What are two pretty ladies like yourselves after me for?"

"We'd like a quick chat, if you don't mind?" Sara extracted her ID and flipped it open for the man to study.

"Police. Have I done something wrong?"

Sara was used to offenders proclaiming their innocence in front of their friends. "Like I said, we'd like a brief chat. Over here okay?"

Somers shrugged and placed his cue lengthwise on the table. "Excuse me, guys, looks like I'm in demand. Carry on without me, I shouldn't be too long."

Sara smiled and motioned for him to join them at the table in the corner. Once they were all seated, he leaned forward and asked, "What's this all about? I've had a few fines in the past, but I paid them up a while ago. I can't think of anything else I've done wrong."

"We're conducting enquiries into a few crimes that have taken place in the area this week. Would you be willing to come down the station to assist us?"

His brow pulled into a deep frown. "Me? Do I have to?"

"It would be completely voluntary at this stage. However, if you object, then we would be forced to question why."

He held his hands upwards above the table. "Hey, I've got nothing to hide. Not sure what sort of crimes you're talking about, but I'm willing to set aside my day off to help you, if that's what you need."

"We appreciate it. We'll even give you a ride in our police car, how about that?"

"Suits me. How will I get back?"

"We'll drop you back here afterwards if that's what you want. Shall we go?"

The three of them stood and made their way to the door.

"Hey, are you wimping out on us, Somers, or have the pretty ladies made you a better offer?" one of his mates shouted.

"Nah. Assisting with their enquiries, chaps. As you were. I'll be back later."

They drove to the station with Somers whistling a merry tune or three in the back seat. He wasn't giving Sara the impression of being a killer, but she knew that it took a certain type of person to end another person's life. Some people collapsed under the pressure when confronted by the police, while others put on a front that concealed their fear. She was putting Somers in the latter category.

Walking into the station, she asked the desk sergeant, "Do we have an interview room free, Sergeant?"

"Of course, ma'am. Room One is available."

"Thanks. Would you arrange for a member of your team to join us, please? Perhaps they could bring us three cups of coffee as well?" She turned to face Somers. "Do you take sugar?"

Somers grinned. "Three heaped for me."

"Two with one sugar, and one with three for our sweet-toothed interviewee."

"Leave it with me, ma'am."

"If you'd like to come this way, Mr. Somers?" Sara led the way down the narrow hallway and into the interview room. "We're going to tape this conversation, if that's all right with you?"

"Whatever. Hey, every time I've seen folks questioned on TV, they've got a solicitor with them. Why haven't I been given the option?"

"If that's what you want, it's fine by me. Do you have a solicitor in mind?"

"Nah, I was just messing with ya. Like I've said already, I've got nothing to hide."

The three of them pulled out the chairs and sat around the small square table. A male uniformed officer joined them a few minutes later, distributed the drinks and then took up his position along the back wall.

Sara nodded, giving Carla the go-ahead to begin taping the conversation. She gave the usual verbiage of who was present in the room and the date and time the interview was taking place, then handed the reins over to Sara to continue.

"Mr. Somers, first of all, I'd like to say how appreciative we are that you volunteered to come into the station today to be interviewed."

Somers smiled a toothy grin, showing off a few rotten teeth. "You're welcome."

Sara noticed a mischievous glint in his eye when their gazes met. "I'm going to give you a few names. I'd like you to tell me if you recognise those names and in what capacity."

"Fire away."

"Ted and Maureen Flowers."

"Nope, never heard of them," Somers replied without hesitation.

"Linda and Samuel Meredith or their daughter, Geraldine."

He shook his head. "Nope. Ditto, never heard of them."

"Okay, what about Laurence and Tina Haldon?"

His mouth turned down at the sides. "Again, not heard of them. Should I have?"

"Unfortunately, in the past few days, five of those people have lost their lives."

"Really? What was it, a pile-up on the motorway or something?"

"No. They were murdered in their own homes."

He bounced back in his chair, and his jaw dropped open. "What? I don't understand why you're asking if I knew them?"

"We have reason to believe that you know at least one of the couples, Mr Somers."

"That's insane. I've already told you that I don't recognise the names. Maybe I'd know their faces if I saw them, but to be honest with you, unless people are mates who I see frequently down the pub et cetera, then I'm sorry, I'm not very clever about remembering folks' names."

"I have a family picture of the Merediths here. Do you recognise any of them?" Sara slid the photo across the desk.

He furiously shook his head after viewing the photo for a few seconds. "Nope, sorry."

Sara pushed away from the table, screeched her chair on the floor and looked down at his trainers. "Maybe you wouldn't mind telling me where you picked up the blood that is now covering your shoes."

He peered under the table and angled his foot. The blood was clearly visible on the white edge of the sole of his right shoe. "No idea."

"Is that so? It seems fresh to me," Sara insisted.

He clicked his fingers. "Wait. I remember now. I went hunting at the weekend with a mate. We caught a few rabbits and skinned them right away."

Sara tilted her head and smiled. "Does this friend have a name?"

"Of course he does. Jack Smith."

"We'll need his phone number and address so he can corroborate your story."

"Fine. It ain't a story, lady, it's the truth. Get a pen and paper, I'll need to check my phone for the details."

Carla spun her notebook around and flipped it to a clean page then slid it across the table at him. Somers checked his phone, finding his friend's details within a few seconds. He scribbled them down then pushed the notebook back to Carla. "There you go. He'll tell you the truth. We go every Sunday."

"Where?"

"Out on the Roman Road."

"What time do you meet Jack?"

"We always meet up around midday, gives us a chance to get over our Saturday night hangovers."

"Until when?"

"It depends," he replied, shrugging. "Until either of us has had enough or we've caught four rabbits, two each."

"How long has this hunting expedition been going on?"

"About the last six months, give or take a few weeks. We don't do any harm, lady, except to the rabbits. The farmers will tell you we're supplying a valuable service."

"I'm presuming guns are involved?"

"Yep. Hey, I know where this is going...Jack's the one with the licence, not me. I only shoot his guns when I'm in his company. I know how to stay on the right side of the law."

"Glad to hear it. Okay, I have a favour to ask."

"Shoot!"

"Would you allow us to have your shoes for DNA testing?"

"Are you saying you don't believe me?"

"I'm not saying that. If you hand your shoes over and the results came back as expected, then that would ensure you were knocked off our suspect list. Will you help us out?"

"Sure. If that's what it will take to get you off my back. All I'm guilty of is killing a few bunnies. I would never, I could never, take a person's life."

"I appreciate your cooperation in this matter."

Carla withdrew a plastic evidence bag from her pocket. Andy kicked off his shoes, picked them up and handed them to her.

"They might smell a bit rich," he apologised, laughing.

Carla made a face and dropped the trainers into the bag and sealed it.

"What size are you?" Sara asked.

"Ten."

"Constable, can you ask the desk sergeant if he has any size ten shoes going spare for me?"

"Right away, ma'am." The constable rushed out of the room and closed the door behind him.

"I'm sorry we dragged you in here, Mr Somers. I'm sure you can appreciate our situation in the circumstances."

"Hey, it was an easy mistake to make."

"While you're here, maybe you can tell me if you've either heard or seen anything suspicious lately to do with these crimes? Perhaps overheard someone talking down the pub this week?" She realised it was a long shot but knew it would be wrong of her to let him go without asking.

"I hear a lot of talk when I'm down the pub. What I haven't heard is someone openly saying they've murdered another person, let alone five people. Not surprising, right? When was the last time you over-heard someone saying anything along those lines?"

"Point taken. I just thought I'd ask."

The door opened, and the constable walked back in the room carrying a pair of old-style plimsolls. He handed them to Somers, who stared at the shoes in disgust. "Hardly a fair exchange. I can't believe people would be seen dead in these."

"Sorry for the inconvenience."

"No worries. Maybe one of you could drop me back home? I'd rather that than be seen down the pub in these."

"I'm sure that can be arranged. Thank you for assisting us with our enquiries. You're free to go now. We'll get your shoes back to you as soon as possible, I promise."

"No problem. Always keen to help the police with their enquiries if the end result means I clear my name."

The four of them left the room. Sara led the way back up the corri-dor. She stopped off to have a brief chat with the desk sergeant to arrange the promised lift for Somers, said farewell to him and then followed Carla up the stairs to the incident room.

After a trip to visit the vending machine, Sara perched herself on the desk closest to Carla. "He seemed genuine enough. Of course, I've come across his type before. Does his best to cover his tracks with a bit of added charm."

"I don't know. I have to say I believe him. It would be daft to spend too much time seeing if his alibi checks out."

"I agree. Will you ring his mate for me, and we'll leave it at that? I'll send the shoes off to forensics just in case—rather that than end up with egg on my face." Sara launched herself off the desk and circulated the room to see how the other members of her team were doing with the tasks she'd handed out.

Christine and Scott were in the process of sifting through the calls they had received.

"Anything useful?" she asked.

Christine shook her head. "The usual names cropping up when a major crime is aired, ma'am. Nothing more than that springing to mind at present."

"That's disappointing. I thought we'd at least get a sighting or something along those lines."

"Maybe the right people missed the appeal, boss," Scott suggested.

"You're probably right. I'll get on to the media, make sure they run the appeal, or at least a section of it, again." She moved round the room to Will and Marissa. "Any good on the house-to-house enquiries at the Haldons', guys?"

Marissa flipped open her notebook. "We took down the statement of the neighbour who reported the crime. He didn't see anyone lingering around outside the property. Unfortunately, his lounge is at the rear of the house, which accounts for why he only saw the Haldons' front door open when he was putting his rubbish out."

"That's a shame. What about the other neighbours?"

"Nothing, boss. Not a scream or a shout heard by any of them," Will said, shrugging.

"I'm not surprised about that, considering they were both discovered with tape wrapped around their mouths. That reminds me, I need to chase up how Mr Haldon is doing in hospital."

"Do you want me to ring the hospital, boss?" Marissa offered.

"Thanks. Let me know as soon as you find out." She moved on to the final pairing of Barry and Jill. "Please tell me you've found a connection between the families?"

"Only that they attended the same church, boss," Jill replied.

"Is that the connection? It seems odd to me. If the killer met them at the church, would he then go on to kill, or attempt to kill, in Laurence Haldon's case? It's a perplexing one, for sure. We could do with something significant coming our way soon before the damn killer strikes again."

"Would it be worth putting on extra patrols in the evening around these villages, boss?" Barry said.

"I actioned that after the first murder took place. I'll ensure the desk sergeant is still sending the patrols out there. Sod the funding for once, we have a killer on the loose who we need to apprehend ASAP. I think that out-trumps any funding restrictions we have in place at the moment. Keep digging, guys. Let me know if anything else crops up."

Thankfully, that night, there were no more murders to report. The following day was spent going over things until the repetitiveness of the conversations became borderline boring with nothing of significance emerging at all. It had been a long week; some days had meant Sara had spent almost twenty hours at work. She was looking forward to putting her feet up over the weekend.

CHAPTER 19

At exactly eleven a.m. on the Friday morning, Mick and his team of heavies arrived on his doorstep. He opened the door and backed up into the lounge, allowing them access into his small rented home.

Mick eyed him cautiously. "Well? Have you got my money?"

He smiled, nodded and crossed the room to the TV cabinet in the corner. Opening the drawer, he removed a plastic carrier bag and held it out to Mick.

Mick snapped his fingers, indicating one of his henchmen to take the bag. The goon snatched it from his hand and tipped the contents out onto the floor and proceeded to count every bundle. A tense silence descended. The goon eventually glanced up at his boss and nodded.

"Looks like it's all here."

Mick inclined his head to one side. He seemed stunned by the announcement. "How? A few days ago you barely had two pennies to rub together, and now you're paying off the full twenty grand. How is that possible?"

"I have good friends who came to my aid when I most needed them," he lied.

"If you expect me to believe that bullshit, you've got another think coming."

"What does it matter? You've got your cash. Now you can call off your heavy mob and fuck off out of my life."

Mick took a few steps towards him. "You might want to curb that foul tongue of yours in my presence. I've got a proposition to put to you."

"You have? What might that be?"

Mick stepped back and flopped onto the sofa. "You get me more of that money, and I'll give you a cut of my business."

He shook his head, resisting the temptation to laugh in the man's face. "Nah. I got the money for you. That should be the end of it."

Mick's gaze narrowed. "You're turning me down?"

He nodded. "I'm moving on soon. Had enough of this area. Need to find another patch where I can put down roots again. Too many memories around here that I'd rather forget, man."

"Sounds like you're running away. From me, for instance."

"I'm not. I'm done with all of this shit. Mick, I've paid you your dough. To me, that's the end of it."

Mick rose from the sofa and walked to within a few inches of him. "The thing is, it's up to me what you do next, not *you*. Yes, you've paid off your debt, but scum like you will always need a backup plan for when your pockets run dry again. Correct?"

"No. I've told you. Things are going to change in the future. I just needed to catch a break to get things on the right track, that's all."

"And your friends came good at the last minute I'm being led to believe?"

He nodded. "That's right. I'd rather pay them back than you; less interest to find that way."

"Are you insulting me and the way I run my business, dickhead?"

"No, man. You're entitled to run your business how you see fit. All I'm saying is that I'm done with this way of life. I'm getting my act together in another area where my face isn't known."

"You're running away. Why? Tell me how you got hold of this money in such a short period of time. I want in."

"Believe me when I tell you, you wouldn't want to be part of it, I promise you."

"Did you bump someone off?"

He swallowed hard, immediately giving himself away.

"What? So you're telling me this is blood money?"

"Whatever, man. You've got your money, just be thankful about that."

"I've had it with you. You make me sick with your holier-than-thou attitude. You've robbed people of their lives and seem so blasé about it. My boys are going to teach you a lesson you won't forget in a hurry, you despicable dirtbag."

"Why? You've got no right to do this. I paid what I owed, and that should be the end of it, Mick. Don't do this, I'm begging you."

Mick smiled, picked up the carrier bag and left the house, leaving behind his two goons who quickly set about him, striking him with powerful hard blows to his stomach and face until everything went black.

CHAPTER 20

S aturday consisted of a leisurely lie-in with Misty stretched out on the bed by her side, a light lunch sitting in the garden with the sun's rays warming her face, followed by a run along the country lanes around the village. She regretted not taking the plunge to take her run before she'd considered filling herself up with lunch. *Idiot!* Indigestion kept her glued to the couch the rest of the day while she caught up on a few of her favourite series she had recorded during the week.

Her mobile rang while she was in the middle of a new episode of *The Great British Bake Off.* The caller ID on her mobile flagged up that it was her mother-in-law, Charlotte, calling. She groaned and rolled her eyes. "Hi, Charlotte. How are things?"

"Hello, dear. Thought I'd better check in with you as you hadn't bothered to contact us in a while."

"Sorry. I meant to ring you last week, but things got on top of me at work."

"No doubt about that, dear, but one must always make time for family. You know I always regard you as family, even though Philip is sadly no longer with us."

"I know, Charlotte. Honestly, you really don't want to know the hours I've put in at work this week."

She sniffled. "I saw you on TV doing that appeal. Those poor families. Has it been hard for you coping with these crimes?"

"I can't lie, it hasn't been easy. I miss Philip every minute of every day still, I always will."

"I appreciate that, dear. That's why it would be nice to see you. Jonathon doesn't understand my need to keep Philip's memory alive—it must be a man thing—but you understand, don't you?"

Sara placed her hand over the mouthpiece of the phone and sighed heavily as her emotions churned. She gulped down the lump that had formed in her throat and dropped her hand. "I understand the need not to forget, I also think there comes a time when we need to move on, Charlotte. It's not doing either of us any good dwelling on what might have been. I was there at the end, and there was nothing anyone could have done to save him. I tried—boy, did I try."

Charlotte was silent for a few moments. It sounded as though her mother-in-law blew her nose a couple of times. "It's so hard for me to contemplate that I'll never see him again. Why can't my husband feel the same way I do? Why? He says the same as you, that we need to move on, but I *can't* do it. I loved Philip with every beat of my heart."

"Everyone knows how different a mother's love is to other members of a family. Charlotte, Jonathon loved Philip as much as you did, it's just different. Men show their feelings differently to us women, but it doesn't mean that he cares any less than we do."

"I need to talk about my grief, and he refuses to listen. That's why I'd like you to come for a visit, so we can reminisce together. To keep his memory from vanishing into oblivion."

"It won't. You're surrounded by his pictures throughout your home. He's with you there, in your mind and in your heart. That will never change, Charlotte. Honestly, once this case is over, I'll do my very best to come and see you, I promise."

She sniffled again. "Okay, I'll have to take your word on that. I'll leave you to enjoy your weekend."

Sara winced at the dig. She felt the need to retaliate. "Hardly enjoying myself. I'm doing the chores that I neglect to do all week. I'll be in touch when things quieten down a little. Take care, Charlotte."

"I'll hold you to that. I've found a nice little restaurant in Cheltenham whilst I was out with the girls the other day. Maybe we'll go there for a treat, yes?"

"Sounds wonderful. I'll be in touch soon. Thanks for ringing." Sara hung up and exhaled a large breath. She felt guilty for fobbing off her mother-in-law the way she had, but there was a world of difference between them. Charlotte had always been a lady who lunches, never worked a day in her life since she'd married Jonathon almost forty years ago. She was a lovely lady who was somewhat overpowering and could only be tolerated in small doses. Philip had felt the same way about his mother when he'd been alive, which was why he'd preferred to live over a hundred miles away from his childhood home. Her mother-in-law's call stirred up old memories she had, up until now, stored away. They had spent the first Christmas of their married life with his mother and father, and Philip had been on tenterhooks the whole time. The truth was, his mother had neglected to treat them both as adults with minds of their own. Sara had analysed that Christmas and had come to the conclusion that Philip was a different person when he was around his mother. It was as if she smothered him by loving him too much, if that was at all possible.

She reflected what life was with her own parents. They were the total opposite to the way Charlotte treated her. They were proud parents, there was no denying that; however, they had always stepped back and allowed Sara to make her own decisions in life, never interfered at all. She had turned to her parents when Philip had died, and they had given her plenty of compassion but had also given her the space she had needed to grieve properly. Unlike Charlotte. Right after Philip's death, and up until his cremation, her mother-in-law had rung her every single day, openly crying on the phone, causing Sara to cry with her. Thinking back, Sara now understood this was the reason her life had stagnated for months. It wasn't until her parents put the idea to her that it would be better for her if she left Liverpool and moved closer to home that she'd even contemplated the notion. Although in moving nearer to her parents, she'd also unwittingly moved closer to Philip's parents in the process.

She couldn't help wondering if that might come back to haunt her one day. There was also the issue that Donald had started sniffing around, too. She liked him; however, if ever things developed between them, she would always have a nagging doubt whether she was with him because he was simply Philip's brother and if she was possibly trying to cling on to a past she was having trouble forgetting.

There was no way she could ever get involved with Donald. What on earth would Charlotte say for a start?

She poured herself a glass of wine and snuggled up with Misty. No, she was happy being alone, for now, in her new home, with her wonderful parents only a phone call away and a dedicated team at work who often made her look good to her superiors. What more could she want in this life? Tears blurred her vision. Philip by her side, that's what. A truly exceptional man who could never be replaced. She wondered how other widows got on with their lives. How long it took them to get over their husband's death. The truth was, she wasn't sure if she'd ever really want to get over losing her soulmate.

CHAPTER 21

The following day, Sara went for a longer run around the village that took her down the public footpaths through a few of the local farmers' fields. She felt invigorated by the end of her run when she showered the sweat from her glowing skin. Sara dried her hair and applied minimal makeup then slipped a summer dress over her head Philip had loved. After feeding Misty and hugging her tight, she left the house and drove to her parents' house for lunch as planned.

"Hello, darling. You look lovely. Any reason you made a special effort today?" her mother asked, basting the chicken.

Sara pecked her mother on the cheek and gave her the bunch of flowers she'd stopped off to buy en route. "No reason, Mum. Fed up wearing trousers or jeans all week, that's all. These are for you. I bought a bottle of white wine as well, guessed we'd be having chicken."

Her mother laughed. "Sorry to be so predictable with lunch."

"Don't be. I thought you'd change your mind about having the beef, knowing how unfair it would be on Dad. I love your roast chicken dinners. Are we having stuffing, too?"

"Of course. Why don't you pop out and see your father? He's in the garden, staking up some of the plants."

Sara walked through the conservatory and out into the garden, little Ethel, her mother's pug, snapping at her heels.

"Hello, love. Ethel, will you stop doing that! One of these days you're going to trip someone up and put them in hospital. Almost did that to me last week, wretched thing."

Sara laughed and kissed her father on the cheek. "She's all right, Dad. How are you? Have you been for more tests lately?"

"Same old, same old, love. The heart's still beating. Some days are better than others. Due to have another check-up next month with yet another consultant."

Sara's own heart squeezed with pain. "You should be taking it easy then."

"Pottering around in the garden won't do me any harm. The doctors advise gentle exercise, so I'm all right doing what I do best out here. You look nice today."

Sara's cheeks warmed under his gaze. "Nice to make an effort for the ones you love now and again, Dad."

"That's lovely to hear. How's that house of yours? I hope you're opening the windows to let it breathe. You know what these new-builds are like."

"I am, Dad. It's a little difficult doing that during the day when I'm at work, but I make sure the windows are open in the evening when I'm at home."

"Good. You hear so many horror stories."

"Your trouble is that you worry too much. I'm going to see if Mum needs a hand with the dinner. Ethel, come on, girl. I'll take her in, out of your way."

"Thanks for that. I'll be in shortly. Just got a few more plants to secure. Never know when a fierce wind is going to strike up."

"I'll leave you to it."

The rest of the day was spent chatting and laughing with her parents, a sharp contrast to the maudlin phone call she'd had with Charlotte the day before.

"Have you heard from Philip's family at all?" her mother asked out of the blue.

"I received a call from his mum yesterday. She's still not coping well."

"You know why that is," her father piped up.

"Why's that, Dad?"

"Because she's sat around the house on her backside all day instead of getting out there occupying her mind by working."

Sara giggled. "She hardly does that, Dad. She's a lady who lunches and attends several charity functions, don't you know? She'll tell you how much she's accomplished, raising thousands, if not millions, towards good causes over the years."

"That's as may be, but even so. She needs to get out more and get on with her life before it passes her by."

"Dad, she's only just turned sixty. She's hardly past it."

"Now, Stephen, stop being so wicked. Leave the poor woman alone."

"I will if she promises to leave Sara alone. No one upsets my daughter and gets away with it."

"I never said she upset me, Dad—well, not intentionally. Sometimes she rings up to chat and stirs up memories I've successfully locked away. She's still grieving and believes I'm in the same place. I'm not; at least, I don't think I am. I have the odd nightmare that I have to deal with, but surely that's natural given the circumstances, right?"

Her mother patted her on the back of the hand. "Of course it's natural, dear."

"Anyway, enough of this maudlin talk. What's happening with you guys? Have you been anywhere exciting this week?" Her parents shared a concerned look. "All right, no holding back, what's wrong?"

"Nothing is wrong per se. It's just Father has had a few twinges that have kept us at home this week as a precaution."

"With your heart, Dad?" she asked, worried.

"Now, stop this. I only admitted to your mother that I was feeling a bit off-colour because I knew how pointless it was hiding the truth. I'll ring the doctor tomorrow, see if he can fit me in for an appointment."

Sara wagged her finger. "Make sure you do. Ring me as soon as you've made the appointment, you hear me?"

"Yes, Mum," he replied sarcastically.

Sara looked up at the clock on the wall. "I better get going soon. Misty will think I've run out on her otherwise."

Her mother left the room and returned with a bulging carrier bag. "Just a few things from the garden, veggies to keep you going."

"Aww...thanks, Mum." She peered into the bag at the wondrous vegetables her parents had grown. "Wow, these look fantastic. I hope my cooking can do them justice."

"If nothing else, it'll make sure you eat proper meals during the week," her father said.

Sara smiled, knowing full well the veggies would probably remain in the bottom of her fridge until the following weekend, unless a miracle should happen in the meantime that would help solve the case and shorten her hours. Her parents had no idea how her working day panned out most of the time—neither did she really, from day to day.

After kissing her parents farewell, Sara left the house. A few minutes into her journey home, something drew her attention in one of the back roads close to her parents' house. A small group of people were gathered along the hedgerow, around a coloured object, something that Sara couldn't quite make out from her position. She parked the car in a nearby lay-by, got out of the vehicle and approached the crowd.

"Evening all. Everything all right here?"

"Aren't you Elizabeth and Stephen's daughter, the policewoman?" a petite woman in her sixties asked.

"That's right. What's wrong? What have you found?"

Two members of the group stood aside, giving her room to see the item. It was a red suitcase that was lying open.

"She's dead," one of the men mumbled.

Sara took a few steps forward to survey the contents closer. Inside, was a small woman with long black hair. The body was intact. Her face was badly bruised, but there was no visible sign of decomposition. "Okay, ladies and gents, I'm going to have to ask you to take a few steps back. This is now a crime scene. Please don't go anywhere. I'll need to take a statement from each of you before you leave. Let me place a few calls first, and I'll be right with you. First of all, I need to know if anyone saw who dumped the suitcase here. A strange car in the area acting suspiciously perhaps? Anything along those lines would help the investigation from the outset."

"Nothing. Old Thomas found the case and alerted a couple of us." An elderly man pointed at another elderly gentleman in the crowd whose gaze was fixed on the girl lying in the case.

Sara tugged on the sleeve of his jacket. "Sir, how long ago did you find her?"

"About an hour, I suppose. Who'd do that to such a beautiful woman?" he asked, his voice trembling.

"I don't know, sir. But I intend to find out. Did you call 999 to report it?"

He turned to look at her and shook his head. "I'm sorry, the thought never entered my mind."

"No problem. Can you take a step back for me, Thomas? Stand alongside the others while I take a look, if you will?"

The man shuffled backwards a few feet to stand with his friends. Under the group's inquisitive gazes, Sara bent down to inspect the corpse without touching either the victim or the case. She could detect a slight decomposing smell, hinting that the woman had possibly been dead for a few days.

Sara stood again and went into full inspector mode. She rang the station first, arranged for the duty sergeant to send the closest squad car he had to the location, and then she rang Lorraine on her direct number.

"Hi, sorry to disturb you on a Sunday, Lorraine."

"No problem, Sara. What can I do for you? And no, the DNA results aren't back from the shoes yet. You'll be the first to hear when they are."

"It's not about that, but thanks, I appreciate it. Umm…I'm out in the country lanes close to my parents' house, and I've just stumbled across something that you should come out and see."

"That's a tad evasive. Care to elucidate for me?"

She turned her back on the crowd and spoke quietly. "I've got the body of a woman that was stored in a large suitcase."

"Jesus! Okay, you've grabbed my attention. Give me the location. I'll get over there right away. Good job I hadn't started on the bottle of wine I promised myself this evening."

She gave her location. "I'll stick around and wait for you."

"See you in about twenty minutes, give or take."

Sara ended the call and returned to inform the crowd that backup would be arriving soon.

While they waited, the group bombarded her with questions about the girl in the suitcase, which she struggled to answer, obviously, as well as questions about the other crimes that had taken place in the area.

Sara truthfully answered most of their questions before asking some of her own. "Has anyone heard anything regarding the other cases? Maybe overheard someone talking about something down the pub?"

Blank stares and shakes of the head greeted her. The usual response, not that she had expected anything else.

It wasn't long before the squad car arrived. She instructed the two PCs to take down everyone's name and address and their statement. Sara removed a pair of latex gloves from her car and returned to the suitcase. She snapped a few photos of the woman, gently pulling her hair away from her battered face.

"I hope you're not interfering with the corpse, Inspector." A stern voice behind almost had her jumping out of her skin.

Sara turned to find Lorraine standing behind her, snapping on a pair of latex gloves of her own. She stepped back to allow the pathologist room to assess the corpse.

"Who found her?"

"One of the gents in the group. My guys are taking down their statements now. They're all pretty shaken up."

"I'm not surprised. Why? Why dump her out here?"

Sara shrugged. "That's just one of many questions I need an answer to. Can you give me a guesstimate of how long you think she's been dead?"

"Roughly, anything between a few days and a week, judging by the smell. The usual—I'll be able to give you a definitive answer once I've opened her up."

"I've taken some photos. I'll run her through the missing persons database at the station in the morning."

"What? You get me to come out on my day off and you're talking about delaying searching for an ID until tomorrow?"

Guilt shrouded her until Lorraine chuckled. "God, you had me going there. You know me, I'll probably start up my computer when I get home anyway. Search through a few news articles et cetera to try and find out who she is."

"Good idea. She's not going anywhere. Another twelve hours or so won't make a difference."

"What drives someone to kill, dump the body in a suitcase and leave it by the side of the road for people to find? They're either careless or they're intent on giving the police the runaround."

"There's another option you neglected to mention."

"What's that?" Sara asked.

"Maybe the killer is trying to get caught."

Sara placed her thumb and forefinger around her chin. "Possibly. It wouldn't be the first time we've stumbled upon something like that, right?"

"Exactly. The last case was only last year if I remember correctly."

"Either way, I need to get an ID for the woman, and soon. Her family must be going out of their minds."

"Not wrong there, I suspect. My team should be here soon. Any chance we can get these guys pushed back farther? It looks like rain. My team will need to erect a marquee. You might want to consider blocking the road off in the meantime."

"I'll organise that with the station now. Be right back." Sara called one of the PCs over. "The pathologist could do with some room to carry out a proper examination. Do you have what you need from the witnesses?"

"We're questioning the last person now, ma'am. Do you want us to release the group then?"

"Yes, let's get this place clear within the next five minutes." She dismissed the constable and placed another call to the station. "We need to block the road off to allow the pathologist and her team to assess the body. Can you organise that for me, Sergeant?"

"I had already taken the liberty of arranging that, ma'am. Reinforcements should be with you soon; they've been given their instructions."

"Excellent news. Thanks. I'll wait for them to arrive before I head off."

"Okay, ma'am. See you tomorrow."

Sara joined Lorraine again. She was observing the ground around the suitcase.

"Waste of time searching for clues there." Sara lowered her voice to add, "These guys were all over the area when I arrived. Not sure they realised what they were looking at, if I'm honest."

Lorraine tutted. "A dead body in a suitcase would definitely send an alert to my brain."

"Yep, mine, too. However, we're not the general public, are we?"

"True. Ah, here come my guys now. Just in time by the looks of things." Lorraine glanced skywards and held her palm up.

"You know why it's raining?" Sara asked.

"Because of the dark cloud formation above us," Lorraine replied logically.

Sara held her hands out to the sides. "That and because I'm wearing a damn summer dress. Go figure."

Lorraine sniggered. "I was going to ask if you'd been on a date."

"Yeah, with my mother and father. Okay, I'm going to leave you to it then. The crowd should be dispersing soon enough. I'll give you a ring in the morning."

"She'll be my top priority, I promise you. Have a good evening."

Sara bid her colleagues farewell and jumped back in her car. Two minutes later, she was inserting her key in the front door and being accosted by Misty the second she stepped foot inside the house.

She swept the cat up into her arms, snuggled and made a fuss of her for the next few minutes and then went into the lounge and immediately booted up her laptop. She wouldn't be able to access the missing persons files they had at the station, but there was a national database open for the general public she could look through for now. Plus, she could use the archives of the online newspapers to hopefully gain an ID for the victim.

Armed with a large glass of white wine, she began the onerous task she'd set herself. By the time ten o'clock came around, her eyes were sore from staring intently at the screen. She retired for the evening, feeling she had let the woman down.

CHAPTER 22

S he must have been exhausted because Sara slept straight
through the night, the first time in weeks she'd managed to
accomplish such a feat.

After feeding Misty, she bolted down a quick slice of toast and
marmalade and a small cup of coffee and raced into work. She was the
first to arrive and took the liberty of switching on all the computers,
anxious to get the team to work on the cases they were handling as
soon as they arrived.

Grabbing a cup of coffee, she took it through to her office and
sorted through her post for the next ten minutes until voices babbled in
the outer office.

"Morning, boss. Any reason all the computer screens are on?"
Carla asked, poking her head into the room.

"Eager to get you guys on the treadmill. Take a seat for a second."

Carla frowned and sat opposite her. "Have I done something
wrong?"

Sara waved a hand in front of her. "Don't be ridiculous. We've got
another case we need to delve into."

Carla sat forward in her chair. "Another murder?"

"Yes, nothing along the lines we've been dealing with." She briefly ran down what had happened on her way home from her parents' the day before.

"What? A girl in a suitcase?"

"More like a woman." Sara picked up her mobile and punched in her password. "Here you go. I tried to search through the missing persons available online but couldn't find her."

"Maybe she's been missing a while and altered her appearance. Dyed her hair perhaps?" Carla shrugged, appearing to doubt her own opinion.

"Possibly. I want the rest of the team to stick with the other cases. You and I need to concentrate on finding out who this woman is. I'm going to take a trip to Mis Pers myself after I've dealt with this lot. I need the woman IDd ASAP."

"What are the chances that there's a connection?"

"It's a long shot. Different MO. All the other victims are of an older generation for a start."

"Maybe he got bored and decided to up the ante after the appeal was aired. Just a suggestion, nothing set in stone, of course. Don't forget he abducted Geraldine."

"True enough. I might be speaking out of turn here, but the pathologist seems to think she possibly died before the appeal went out."

"Maybe she is connected to him and spoke out of turn."

"As in, she was his girlfriend?"

"I don't know. It just seems odd that the suitcase was dumped in the centre of the area where all the other murders took place. Plus, there's the fact that we're not used to dealing with murder enquiries on our patch."

Sara pointed at her partner. "You could have a point there. Let's work along those lines for now until something turns up to dismiss that theory."

Carla smiled and jumped to her feet. "I'll start cracking the whip."

She left Sara completing her chores. Halfway through, Sara picked up the phone and rang the Missing Persons Department. "Maddy, hi, it's Sara Ramsey. Is it possible to pop along and see you on an urgent matter?"

"Of course. There's nothing that important sitting on my desk right now that can't be set aside for a few minutes. To do with a missing person?"

"Yes, unfortunately. I'll tell you all about it when I see you. Won't be long." Sara hung up. She gathered her notebook and pen, snatched up her phone and rushed out of the office. "Carla, we've got an appointment to keep."

Carla scraped her chair and trotted to keep up with her as they headed up a flight of stairs to the next level.

Maddy was sitting at her desk and smiled when they entered her office. "Hello, you two. Pull up a chair. Now, what can I do for you?"

Sara held out her phone for Maddy to see. "It's not gruesome, I promise."

Maddy's hand covered her cheek, and she shook her head, visibly distressed by the photo. "Oh my. That poor woman. Was she found in that suitcase?"

"She was. I wondered if you recognised her. I know it's a long shot but I thought it was worth a punt. If anyone is likely to recognise her, it's you, right?"

"Well, I do spend a majority of my time trawling through the images on our database. Give me a second." She twisted the phone in different directions, sourcing a better angle. "I take it she was found in this area?"

"Sorry, I should have said. Yes, out near my neck of the woods, close to Marden."

"Okay, well, that will hopefully narrow it down. Why don't I do a search of all the young women in the area who have been reported missing in the last year? How's that?"

"Sounds perfect." Sara held up her crossed fingers.

Maddy tapped her keyboard and swivelled her monitor so that all three of them could see the screen. "The computer is on slow today, typical hey."

Sara grinned. "I guess we're not the only ones who have the blues on a Monday morning."

Maddy smiled. Sara watched the egg timer in the centre of the screen in an almost hypnotic trance until a dozen or more pictures filled it.

"Ahh, there at last. We've got two pages of people."

"Can we study each person in detail? Carla seems to think the woman may have changed her appearance in some way. I had a brief look through the online Mis Pers database last night, and nothing came to light."

"Let's do that then. Why don't we focus on the woman's facial features? Obviously, her eyes are closed, so we won't be able to identify her from her eye colour, but I hardly think she'll change the shape of her jawline or possibly her nose. Mind you, we'll have to look past all the bruising."

The three of them fell silent while the photos of the missing persons on the screen absorbed their attention. "I can't find anything of use on this page. What about you, guys?" Sara asked.

Carla and Maddy both shook their heads.

"Let's flip the page. Ready to focus again, ladies?" Maddy asked, hitting a button on her keyboard.

A dozen new images appeared on the screen. Sara found her eyes drawn to one particular woman in the centre. She reached for her phone and held the photo of the girl in the suitcase alongside the woman who had drawn her attention. "What do you think?"

"Looks like a clear match to me," Maddy said.

"She's dyed her hair. I had an inkling that would be the case. There are not many genuine black-haired people walking the streets," Carla stated, surprising Sara.

"Really? I suppose you're right. I've never really thought about that before. Can you give us a name, Maddy?"

"Let me do that for you now." Her fingers worked nonstop until the printer sparked into life beside her. She withdrew the paper from the tray and handed it to Sara. "Everything you need to know should be on there for you."

Sara checked the sheet of paper and punched the air, delighted their trip had been worthwhile for a change. "You're brilliant. Thanks for your help, Maddy."

"Always a pleasure, even if the circumstances turn out to be the sad variety as in this case. At least the family will have closure now."

"There is that. Thanks, Maddy. See you soon."

Sara and Carla rushed out of the office and back down the stairs. "We need to go and visit her next of kin," Sara said, sighing heavily.

"Now?"

"Yep, let me drop by and tell the others what we've found out first." She pushed through the incident room door, recapped what they had learnt from Maddy and put Jill in charge of carrying out a background check on the woman. "We'll see you later."

Sara and Carla left the station. They arrived at Dawn Dawson's mother's house on the edge of the city at Tupsley around ten minutes later.

Sara prepared herself for the trauma she was aware that lay ahead of them and rang the bell.

A woman with a warm smile whom Sara guessed to be in her fifties opened the door. "Hello, can I help?"

Sara and Carla held up their warrant cards. "Hello, Mrs Dawson. Would it be all right if we come in and spoke to you for a moment?"

She clutched the edges of her cardigan, and her eyes widened. "Have you found her, Dawn?"

Sara nodded. "It would be better if we didn't do this out here."

Mrs Dawson pulled the door open and pushed herself back against the wall. "She's dead, isn't she? My baby is dead!"

Sara nodded. "I'm so sorry."

Mrs Dawson covered her face with both hands and sobbed. Sara gulped down the emotions threatening to emerge. *Why is this part of the job so difficult?* "Is there anyone else at home?"

Shaking her head, Mrs Dawson led the way into the lounge. She sat on the edge of the sofa. "My husband is away on business, he's not due back for another few days. Where? Where did you find her? Has she been assaulted? Please tell me she hasn't."

"I don't believe she's been sexually assaulted, although the pathologist has yet to perform a postmortem. That will be conducted today. I have to tell you that I was there when your daughter's body was discovered. She was found in a suitcase."

"What do you mean by that?"

"Just that. Someone placed your daughter's body in a suitcase and left it lying on the side of the road."

"For what reason? How heartless can people be?"

Sara shrugged. "I'm sorry. The forensics team will search the area and examine the suitcase thoroughly, looking for any clues to help us ID the person. Until that happens, we'll be interviewing people who have been connected to Dawn in recent months, if we can find anyone. I'll put out an appeal later for anyone who knew her. Hopefully we'll be able to piece together what has happened to her since you reported her missing. That was five months ago, is that correct?"

"Yes. We used to be in regular contact, and then she just stopped ringing me. I went round to the flat she shared with her friend, and she told me that she had moved out."

"Did her friend tell you why?" Sara noted down the answers in her notebook.

"No. Only that she'd started seeing this man recently and she seemed pretty keen on him." She shook her head. "We used to be so close. She either forgot to tell me about the man she was seeing or was too embarrassed to mention him." Fresh tears filled her eyes, and she plucked a tissue out of the box sitting on the table beside her.

"Does that mean you don't know the man's name?"

"That's right. Otherwise I would have informed the police when I reported her missing. I'm as much in the dark about their relationship as you are."

"What about her flatmate, did you ask her?"

"I went round there, but it was pointless. The girl was high on drugs, didn't even know what time of the day it was, let alone anything else I tried to get answers to. I'm hoping that Dawn wasn't into drugs; she was always a dependable young woman, up until she went missing. Once they're out from under your nose, you really don't have a clue what they get up to, do you?" She sniffled and wiped her nose and then her eyes with a fresh part of the tissue.

"Does the name Andy or Andrew Somers ring a bell with you?" Sara asked.

Mrs Dawson thought over the name for a few moments before she replied, "No. I can't say I recognise it. Why? Should I?"

"Not really. We've spoken to a young man by that name in the past few days regarding another crime that has taken place in the area. It was a long shot on my part, if I'm honest with you."

"Maybe her flatmate, or former flatmate, should I say, can help you out about that. God, I hate the thought of her getting involved with someone of that ilk. Obviously she has, somewhere along the line, otherwise she wouldn't be d..." She swallowed loudly and covered her face again.

"I'm sorry, that's quite often the case with these things. We'll get to the bottom of this and punish the person who took your daughter's life, I'll promise you that."

"Thank you. What if they've taken off by now? Will you still be able to find them?"

"We will. As long as we have a name. It's surprising what we can do to find someone. Of course, without a name it makes our job so much harder."

"I can understand that."

"I'm sorry to have to put you out like this, but would it be possible to give us your daughter's previous address? We'll drop by and see what we can find out from her flatmate."

The woman rose from her chair and walked across the room to open a drawer in an oak side cabinet. She withdrew a small address book and returned to her seat. She flipped to a page and stretched out her arm.

Sara took the address book and noted down the information, including the phone number, and handed it back to Mrs Dawson. "Can I ask where your daughter worked?"

"She was a barmaid in town, at the Wetherspoon's pub down by the station." She gasped, "Maybe they can give you what you need to know."

"We'll go and see them during the day. Do you need me to call anyone to come and sit with you?"

"No. I'll be fine once I've had a good cry. Truth be told, I'm all cried out. I had a feeling someone would knock on my door one day with disastrous news. It was inevitable, I suppose."

"I'm sorry for your loss. We'd better get the investigation underway."

Mrs Dawson showed them to the front door and shook their hands. "Please, do all you can to get Dawn the justice she deserves."

"We'll do our very best. I'll be in touch with you soon with our progress."

CHAPTER 23

S ara decided, as the pub was closer, to drop in there first. The lunchtime rush was about to get underway. "Fancy a sandwich?"

Carla nodded. "Why not? We've got to eat, right?"

"I'll place the order and ask the manager to come and see us when he has a spare few minutes. It'll take the pressure off him then. What do you fancy?"

"This is on me, remember?" Carla insisted. She grabbed the menu off the bar and ran her finger down it. "I fancy a chicken and salad baguette. What about you?"

"Make it two. I'll have a small OJ as well, please." She took out a tenner from her purse, but Carla shoved her hand away. Sara tutted and went to the other end of the bar to try to locate the manager.

She walked up to a youngish man whom she had seen issuing orders and took that to mean he was the manager. "Hi, I appreciate how busy you are." She flashed her ID. "I'd like a brief chat if it's not too much trouble. We've ordered lunch, so we'll be around for the next half an hour or so anyway."

"Can I ask what this is about? We don't get a lot of trouble in here, not lately."

"About a former employee of yours, Dawn Dawson."

His brow furrowed. "Now that's a name I haven't heard for a few months. Okay, I don't know much. Give me ten minutes. Enjoy your meal in the meantime."

"Thanks." Sara smiled and rejoined Carla who was placing their order.

"Everything all right? From a distance he didn't seem that enamoured about us being here."

"He was fine. Stressed, that's all. He'll join us in a few minutes. Where do you want to sit?"

Carla pointed away from the crowd of diners over to a spare table close to the window. "Looks ideal over there."

They took their drinks and made their way over to the table before anyone else beat them to it.

"Cheers," Sara said, chinking her glass against her partner's.

After taking a sip of the cold orange juice, Carla asked, "What do you think is going on then?"

Sara shrugged. "It's looking more and more like the fella she was involved with is possibly behind her murder. Not sure what else we can say about her circumstances yet, not until we've spoken to the manager and the flatmate. Let's hope the flatmate is around today. I'd like to wrap this up and get back to the other cases we're dealing with swiftly."

"Someone has to know something. One thing that's bugging me."

"Go on," Sara said.

"If she was that close to her mother, why hasn't she been in contact with her for the past five months? There's no way her body had been in that suitcase all that time, so where has she been?"

"Maybe this man abducted her, kept her prisoner and then got rid of her."

"Hmm...maybe. I know if I was close to my mum and in trouble, I'd do everything in my power to try and get word to her, if only to put her mind at rest that I was alive."

"Me, too. Which makes me think she was being held against her will, possibly."

The waitress arrived and placed their large baguettes in front of them. "Thanks. Crikey, maybe we should have shared one," Sara said, lifting up the side of the roll to see the contents.

Carla chuckled. "I think you're right. I'll never get through this. Shame I haven't got a dog, I could have asked for a doggie bag."

Sara laughed. "Don't say that. My bloody mother does that every time we go out. Either that or she nicks a serviette off the next table and places her leftovers in it."

"Never! Mums can be so funny at times, can't they?"

"Yep, I suppose so. I wouldn't be without mine, though."

"True. Mum and I really get on, too. She's prone to interfering in my love life now and again, but that's what mums do, right?"

"Mine never has. I guess I'm lucky on that front. She trusts me to do the right thing."

"Did your parents get on well with your husband?"

"Yes. They treated him as if he were their own flesh and blood."

"That's wonderful. So sad you lost him at such a young age. Sorry, I know you don't want to talk about it, ignore me."

"It's fine. I suppose I'm still very raw. I loved the very bones of that man. I always thought people who said that didn't really know what they were saying, but it's a great description when you actually share your life with your soulmate." She took a bite from her baguette and felt relieved when she saw the manager striding towards them.

"Can we make this quick?" He drew up a chair and sat alongside Sara.

She wiped her mouth on her napkin and took out her notebook. "Of course. How long did Dawn work for you?"

"About a year on and off. She left for a few weeks but then pleaded with me to take her on again. She was a good worker, so I had no hesitation giving her another chance."

"We've heard that she was involved with a man not long before she was reported missing. Did that man ever come in here?"

"He did once or twice. I wasn't too happy about it. Looked a nice enough chap, but I can't abide the staff fraternising with people they know when they should be working." He held his hand up. "You can see how busy this place gets, it's even worse in the evenings."

"Understandable. I don't suppose you can tell us what his name was?"

He placed a hand on his cheek and turned his head to the side as he thought. "Crap, I can't. I think, but don't quote me on this, that it began with an M."

"Mark, Mick, Michael, Matthew?"

He sighed. "Possibly Matthew, Matt. I'm not sure, though."

"Thanks, we'll note that down. I take it you haven't seen Dawn since she was reported missing?"

"No. Not seen or heard from her for over five months I think it is now." He glanced over his shoulder at the bar and tutted. "The queue is getting long now. Was there anything else?"

"Nothing else. Except that Dawn's body was found yesterday."

"Crap! Body? As in, she's dead?"

"I'm afraid so. Can I give you my card? If you hear anything on the grapevine once the news gets out, will you ring me?"

"Of course I will. That poor girl. I feel terrible now, rushing our meeting. Life really sucks, doesn't it?"

"Sometimes it does. Thanks for taking time out of your busy day to speak to us. Sorry if the news has come as a shock."

"Don't mention it. Her poor family. Her mother used to come in here regularly to see her, never got in the way, so I didn't mind as such. I can't believe anyone would kill her, or did they? You never said that, did you? I'm assuming that's the case."

"We believe so. We'll pass on your condolences to the family when we see them."

"Enjoy the rest of your lunch. Not sure how you can eat dealing with things like this every day."

Sara smiled. "Thankfully, cases like this don't happen that often. When they do, we just have to knuckle down and get on with it."

He nodded and walked away.

By this time, Sara had gone off the lunch sitting in front of her and pushed her half-eaten baguette to one side. Carla had barely come up for air since she'd started eating hers and sighed contentedly when she placed her empty plate underneath Sara's.

"Drink up," Sara said, "we'll nip over to see if the flatmate is in. First I need to ring Jane to set up another media appeal for this afternoon if possible."

"I'd say you're cutting it a bit fine, but it's worth a shot."

However, Jane was far more accommodating than anticipated and said she could probably arrange one for around four that afternoon.

CHAPTER 24

The house was terraced and looked to be in fairly good condition for a rental property. Sara approached the building, which was split into two flats, with trepidation niggling at her insides. She rang the bell. The door was opened quite quickly by a young woman with long plaited blonde hair. She had black rings around her eyes as though she hadn't slept in days.

"Jackie Moore?"

"I am. And you are?"

Sara produced her ID. "DI Sara Ramsey and DS Carla Jameson. Mind if we come in for a brief chat?"

"Do I have a choice? What's this about?" She eyed them warily.

"Yes, you can deny us access, but if you do, you're likely to raise our suspicions."

"You still haven't told me what this is about."

"Your flatmate."

"Teri, what's she done?"

"My mistake, your former flatmate, Dawn."

Her mouth gaped open for a few moments. "Have you found her?"

Sara nodded. "Sadly, yes. Please, it would be better if we did this inside."

She opened the door wider and led them up the stairs to the flat above. The lounge wasn't the tidiest Sara had ever seen, but it wasn't the messiest either.

Jackie cleared some clothes off the sofa so they could sit down. "Are you telling me that she's dead?"

"Yes. We've escalated the case from a missing person to a murder enquiry. Has Dawn contacted you since she went missing?"

"No, nothing at all. She owed me rent, too. I was pretty miffed about that. Feel guilty as hell now, knowing that she's dead. Her body, was it decomposed when you found it? Sorry, I have a morbid fascination with postmortems and corpses, always have had."

"No. By the looks of things, Dawn died fairly recently."

"Shit! Where has she been for the last five or six months then?"

"We're not sure. We're guessing that someone possibly restrained her in some way."

"You mean she was being kept as a sex slave somewhere?"

"You have quite a vivid imagination, Jackie. What do you do for a living?"

"Nothing right now. I'm on the dole. I walked out on my last job; they couldn't fathom me out, they said, so I upped and left."

"What type of work?"

"I had a boring desk job at an accountancy firm as a bookkeeper. I know, I don't look the type. It wasn't my ideal job, but it paid the bills. I'm an artist really. Not much call for art nowadays, not the type of abstract paintings I like to create anyway." She pointed at the wall behind them.

Sara turned to study the painting that was dark in colour and composition. "It's really good."

"I know you're just saying that. I have an eye for the unusual, shall we say?"

"I can't deny that," Sara said, facing the young woman again. "Look, we don't want to keep you long. We're eager to get on with the investigation, but we'd like to ask a few questions, if that's okay?"

"I'll try and answer them, not that I know much. Dawn and I shared a flat but nothing else, if you get my meaning? We kept our distance as far as our private lives were concerned. Maybe if I had taken more interest in her she would have confided in me as to what was going on with that chap of hers."

"That's who we wanted to discuss with you. Do you know where she met him?"

"At the pub where she worked."

"Did she mention his name? Or did you meet him at all?"

"Now you're asking. Hang on, yes, I believe it was Matthew— sorry, can't for the life of me remember what his surname was or if I ever knew it. No, he never came here. We had a rule that we didn't bring members of the opposite sex to the flat, in case it caused any awkwardness between us."

"Any idea where he worked?"

"No, sorry. That's as much as I know about him. Except that Dawn came home with a thick lip one day. I challenged her about where she got it from. She was shifty and said that a punter at the pub had given her a thump. I got the impression she was covering for him. I'm right, yes?"

"If he's the one who killed her, then I'd suggest you had a right to be suspicious of him. Silly girl. She should have trusted someone."

"I told her I thought it was him and that she would be better off dumping him, but she was having none of it. Told me to stop interfering. A few days later, she went missing."

Sara's heart sank. "Such a shame that some people can't detect the signs of an abusive relationship early on when it sticks out like a sore thumb to others."

"I feel guilty that I wasn't able to talk her out of being with him."

"You did your best. Any idea where he lived?"

Jackie shook her head. "No, I don't. Would he still be at the same address?"

"We have to believe he would be, no reason to suspect otherwise. Thanks for all your help. We're going to put out an appeal through the media channels this afternoon. Hopefully it'll prompt people to get in touch with us."

"I hope it does. It's wrong, if he took her life, not to get punished for it."

"If we catch whoever killed her, they'll be put away for years, if not life. Thanks again. Take my card. If anything springs to mind that you think I should know about, don't hesitate to get in touch."

Jackie nodded and placed the card in the back pocket of her jeans then showed them back downstairs.

"What do you make of that?" Carla said, once they were seated in the car and en route back to the station.

"I think, as already suspected, the boyfriend is the guilty party. Now all we have to do is try to find the bastard."

"Are you going to mention his name in the appeal?"

"I was going to. Why? You think that might cause him to run?"

"Possibly. I don't know. I hope someone recognises her picture; we could do with a break."

"Ain't that the truth."

CHAPTER 25

A few hours later, Sara was sitting in front of the media cameras again, appealing to the public for assistance. The story wasn't due to be aired until later that evening, during the local bulletin after the main *News at Ten* slot. Therefore, Sara insisted they should call it a day early in the hope they would be extra busy in the morning, manning the red-hot phones.

She drove home, exhausted, both mentally and physically. The moment she stepped through the front door of her home, her mobile rang. Her heart lurched when Donald's name filled the screen. "Hi, Donald, you've just caught me. I was about to jump in the bath," she lied.

"I could nip over and scrub your back."

She closed her eyes and cringed. "Maybe another time. It's been a hard day at work. What can I do for you?"

"I thought you might fancy going out for a meal or a drink."

She was torn between telling him to piss off and trying to let him down gently. The latter option proved to be the less hurtful and far more tactful. "Maybe another time. Being involved in several murder cases takes its toll on the mind and body. I wouldn't be much company to be honest with you."

There was an awkward silence on the line for a few seconds. She shuddered at the sound of his breathing. "Fair enough. Enjoy your bath," he said abruptly. He ended the call before she could respond.

Instead of feeling guilty, she felt relieved. After removing her shoes, she suddenly realised that Misty hadn't come to the door to greet her, which was unheard of. "Misty, where are you?" Still nothing. Sara rushed upstairs, thinking she might have shut the cat in the bedroom, but no, the bedroom door was wide open. She crossed the room and looked down at the small rear garden that was laid to lawn, but Misty wasn't there either. She ran back down the stairs through the lounge and into the kitchen. There was no sign of her beloved cat.

Fear planted itself firmly in the pit of her stomach. *No, please, let her be all right.* She craned her neck at a faint sound of meowing. She followed the noise, calling Misty's name as she went into the kitchen, and opened the back door. Misty was lying on the back doorstep, foaming at the mouth.

Sara screamed. She grabbed her cat, locked up the house and ran out to the car. She was sitting in the vet's waiting room, desperate to be seen, ten minutes later, tears streaming down her face while she stroked Misty. With each stroke, her cat whimpered in pain. "Please, isn't there anyone else who can see me? I think she's dying," she pleaded with the receptionist.

"I'm sorry. The vet is dealing with another emergency at the moment. Hopefully he won't be too long now."

With that, two people emerged from the room, a little old lady who was sobbing, and a tall young vet who was trying to comfort her, telling her that she had done the right thing in letting her dog go.

Crap! I hope he doesn't expect me to put Misty down. I couldn't do it.

The vet saw the old lady to the door and then turned his attention to Sara and Misty. "Gosh, she looks in a bad way. I apologise for keeping you waiting. Come through."

Sara gently cradled Misty in her arms and followed the vet into his small examination room. He tore off a roll of tissue and sanitised the table then instructed Sara to place Misty down.

"What happened?"

"I don't know. I got in from work about thirty minutes ago. She usually greets me at the door but she didn't. I searched the house and then found her lying on the back doorstep. She was crying out in pain. Please help her."

"I'll do my best. She's going to whimper as I examine her, so please don't think I'm hurting her intentionally."

"Okay. Just to warn you, I'm a police officer." Sara issued him a slight smile.

"I better be doubly careful then. Hello there, Misty. Feeling poorly, are you?"

He laid his hand on Misty's stomach. Her erratic breathing was fiercely inflating her chest. Sara comforted her, gently talking to her while the vet carried out his examination.

"Okay, I believe she's been poisoned."

Sara gasped despite the vet confirming what she already suspected. "Oh no, is there anything you can do for her?"

"We can try and flush out the toxins. I need to prepare you for the worst scenario—most cats don't pull through."

Sara's breath caught in her throat. "Please, please try your best to save her. She's all I've got since I lost my husband." She broke down and kissed Misty on the head.

"I'll do my best. Do you want to leave her with me overnight?"

She sniffled. "Not really. But if that's what I have to do, I'm prepared to do it."

"I promise to take care of her. We need to work quickly before her organs start shutting down."

Sara nodded and walked towards the door. "Will you ring me later?"

"Of course. Leave your mobile number with the receptionist on your way out. Try not to worry too much."

Sara did as instructed and then drove home in a daze. She contemplated dropping in to her parents' house on the way home but decided against it. Once she was home, she made a coffee and sat at the kitchen table, staring at her mobile, willing it to ring. Her wish was granted two hours later when the vet rang.

"Hello there, it's Mark Fisher, the vet. Misty is on a drip. She's in an extremely sorry state; we'll know more in the morning."

"I can sense what you're not saying...there's a possibility that she might die overnight, isn't there?"

"Try to think on the positive side of things. You obtained help as soon as you could. That will go in her favour."

"Maybe. I haven't got a clue how long she was lying there, though."

"Let's put it another way. Another half an hour, and I fear she wouldn't be with us now, so please, don't beat yourself up about this. You've done your best for her. Let's see how she responds in the morning. I'll ring you first thing around eight, okay?"

"Perfect, thank you so much for caring for her, Dr Fisher."

"It's my pleasure. Speak again in the morning. She's in safe hands, I promise. A member of staff will be checking on her throughout the night."

"That's a relief, thank you."

Sara dropped her phone on the table and buried her head in her hands. How? Why? Was it deliberate? Or did Misty pick up something from the site? Too many questions riffled through her mind that she just didn't have the answers to.

She called it a day and let her weary legs transport her upstairs, knowing full well that she wouldn't be able to sleep properly until she knew her baby was better. She switched on her phone and listened to Philip's soothing voice. "Where are you when I need you the most? What if she dies? If you can hear me, watch over her tonight, Philip, she's all I've got. I can't lose her as well as you."

CHAPTER 26

After a fitful night's sleep, Sara was in the shower when her mobile rang. Quickly drying her hand first, she answered it. "Hello. Sara Ramsey."

"Ah, hi. It's Mark Fisher, the vet."

"Oh. Is it good news or bad?"

"It's all good. Misty was sitting up purring when I came in this morning."

"Oh my goodness. I can't tell you what a relief that is to hear you say that. I've been dreading your call all night."

"I'm sure. I told you to have faith. I'd like to keep an eye on her throughout the day just in case she relapses."

"The chances of that happening are?"

"Negligible, but I'd like to be safer than sorry. Can you pick her up on your way home from work this evening?"

"Around six, maybe half past, depending on how the day pans out."

"I understand. Evening surgery is on until eight, so it's up to you when you pick her up."

"I'll be straight there. I'm eager to see her. Give Misty a gentle hug from me. Thank you, Dr Fisher. You've saved more than Misty's life, I assure you."

"No problem. It was my pleasure. However, I believe your prompt actions saved the day. See you later."

Sara smiled and slipped under the shower once more. She even managed to conjure up a little ditty to sing.

She drove into work, her heart feeling lighter than it had the previous evening when she'd been sitting in the waiting room at the vet's.

"Crikey! You look rough," Carla said, the minute she entered the incident room.

"Thanks. I appreciate the compliment. I had a rough evening, and the night was even worse."

"Sit down, I'll get you a drink." Carla rushed over to the vending machine and returned carrying two steaming cups of coffee.

"Thanks, I'll need several cups before I can function properly this morning."

"Are you going to tell me what has happened?"

Sara sighed heavily and told her partner about the drama that had unfolded the evening before. "That's it in a nutshell. Thankfully, Misty has survived the ordeal."

"Bloody hell. Do you think it was deliberate?"

Sara frowned. "I'm not sure. I'm still living on a building site, so maybe she got in somewhere she shouldn't have and lapped up a liquid she thought was water. I don't know. I'm going to ring the site manager today to make him aware of the situation."

"I have another theory if you're willing to listen."

"I'm all ears."

"What if you were targeted by the killer?" Carla suggested, her tone deadly serious.

"You reckon? How would he know where I live?"

"Let's be honest, your face has been all over the news. He's only got to look you up. Maybe he followed you home without you realising it."

"That's a touch Miss Marpleish, even for you."

"More like Midsomer Murders considering you live out in the sticks." Carla laughed. "No. Seriously, you need to consider my theory as a genuine possibility. Glad to hear Misty pulled through in the end."

"I hope so. I can't wait to see her. She's my world, and I'm lost without her sleeping on my bed at night or trying to trip me up when I walk through the door."

"I bet. Such an awful thing to happen. What's on the agenda for today?"

Sara held up a handful of notes the desk sergeant had given her on the way in. "We need to look through these first, see if anything new has come in from either of the appeals we've run. I want to chase up the lab, too. They should have some results in for us soon. It won't hurt to give them a gentle prod."

Carla held out her hand for the notes. "I'll go through these and let you know if anything interesting pops up."

Sara smiled. "Thanks. I better go and tackle the post. Hopefully, it won't take me too long and we can crack on again. Ever get a feeling you're in for a good day even when things are stacked against you?"

"Sometimes. Is that how you feel?"

"Yeah, as though something is going to happen in our favour for a change today."

After dealing with countless brown envelopes, Sara returned to the incident room half an hour later to say good morning to the rest of the team and ask for an update from everyone. The phone on Carla's desk rang as she approached her partner.

"Hello. DS Jameson. How may I help?"

A frown developed on Carla's face, and her head rose slowly to make eye contact with Sara. "What's up?" Sara mouthed.

"I'm just going to put you on speaker if that's all right, so my boss can hear."

Sara placed both hands on Carla's desk and listened to the conversation.

"Just to reiterate," Carla stated, "You're related to Maureen and Ted Flowers."

"Yes. I'm their granddaughter."

"Okay, Mrs Lindon. Please tell us what you know."

The woman appeared to hesitate for an instant, then said, "It's about the appeal that went out last night, about the girl who was murdered, Dawn I think her name was."

"That's right. Do you know her?"

"I've debated whether to ring you or not, but I believe I saw the woman with my ex-husband a few months back at a party."

"Your ex-husband? What's his name?" Carla asked eagerly.

"Matthew Lindon."

Sara and Carla stared at each other as the realisation dawned on both of them. She was right about something decent landing in their laps.

"Hi, Mrs Lindon, this is DI Sara Ramsey. We questioned the rest of your family, but I believe you were away at the beginning of last week."

"That's right. I only got back on Friday. Mum mentioned you were working on the case. I didn't feel the need to ring you when I returned because I didn't have any news for you, not regarding Nan and Granddad anyway."

"Can you tell us more about Matthew?"

"What do you need to know? We're not really in touch now, not since he beat me up. I've kept my distance from him."

"He abused you during your marriage? Did you report it?"

"Yes, it became a daily occurrence. He changed as soon as the wedding band was slipped on his finger. Well, maybe not right away, it took a few months for him to show his true colours. My family made him feel welcome, but it just wasn't enough for him."

"Can you pinpoint why the abuse started?"

"Usually it was about money. He needed it, and I refused to hand over my hard-earned wages. He was in and out of work. I got the impression after a while that he saw me as some sort of meal ticket. I've always worked hard to achieve what I have. I refused to hand over my cash when he walked out on a job, so he beat me up. It was so bad I had to take a few days off work before the swelling went down.

Makeup can cover the bruises—it can't disguise the puffiness that follows a beating, though."

"I see. You kicked him out, I presume, after that?"

"Yep, I couldn't do it alone. Thankfully, a couple of my uncles and my granddad, God rest his soul, came to my rescue and persuaded him to leave."

"And he went willingly?"

"In the end, yes." She gasped. "Oh my God, you don't suppose *he* was the one who killed my grandparents?"

"At this point we don't know. We'll need more to go on than what you've told us already. What about Dawn? Did Matthew introduce you to her?"

"No, nothing like that. We were at a party. I tried my hardest to get some time alone with her, in the ladies' or something, you know, to try and warn her what he was like, but he stuck to her like glue. Had his hand on her arm the whole time, as if he was afraid to let her out of his sight."

"Did she look uncomfortable in his presence?"

"Yes and no. He's a control freak, Inspector. I regret the day I ever got involved with him. If I find out he was behind my grandparents' murders…well, all I can say is that you better get to him first."

"Don't worry, I understand where you're coming from. Now that his name has been highlighted, we'll keep him under observation until any evidence surfaces. Whoever killed your grandparents did their very best not to leave any evidence behind, therefore it's going to be difficult pinning their murder on him unless something substantial comes our way. That doesn't mean to say we're going to discount what you're telling us."

"I'm glad to hear that. He's a menace to society, although to talk to him you'd think he was a decent chap. Get behind the front door with him, and that's when his true colours show."

"Okay, leave it with us, if you will. I appreciate you calling us. Please don't make contact with him. I'd also advise you not telling the rest of your family, in case they decide to take matters into their own hands before we get the chance to pick him up."

"I haven't told them for that very reason."

"Good. One last thing. Do you know where he lives?"

"I'm sorry, I don't."

"Not to worry. We'll do some digging. As soon as I know anything further, I'll contact you. Thanks again, Mrs Lindon."

"It's Mary-Ann, and I'm in the process of reverting back to my maiden name. The sooner that happens the better."

"Speak soon." Sara gestured for Carla to end the call. "Okay, that was interesting. Can you see what you can find out about Matthew Lindon? Let's shake the monkey out of the tree and see if he lands on both feet. Pay special attention to any trouble he's been in in the past."

"Will do. This could be the break we're looking for," Carla said, starting up her computer.

"I said I had a feeling, didn't I? I'll get on to Lorraine, let her know what we're dealing with and urge her to get a move on with the lab results. It would be good if we could link all the cases."

"I'll try and locate his address first. Would it be worth putting a tail on him?"

"Yep, I think that's what we should do, if he hasn't taken flight already. He might have done with all the press coverage on all cases now. Get his address." Sara turned to talk to the rest of the team. "Will and Barry, will you start the surveillance? We'll swap over during the day. Keep digging in the meantime, guys. I sense we're almost there."

She rushed into her office and rang Lorraine. "Hi, it's me. Can you talk?"

"For a moment. What's up?"

"A suspect has been highlighted in the Dawn Dawson case. I need to know if you found anything on the suitcase."

"That's good news. As it happens, yes. We found a partial fingerprint that my guys are running through the system."

"What's taking so long?"

"I know you're eager, but we're at the hands of technology. The system had a blip yesterday and stopped functioning most of the day. A technician worked through the night. We think we're back on track now."

"Great. How long are we looking at? Or is that a daft question?"

"Yep. If you give me the name, I'll ring you as soon as we come up with something."

"Matthew Lindon. We're putting two and two together at the moment and coming up with ten. We think it's likely that he was behind the other murders in the area, too. He's the ex-husband of the first victims' granddaughter."

"Whoa! Really?"

"Yep. We're doing checks on him now. I hate to hurry you…"

"But you're going to anyway. Leave it with me. I'll have a chat with my team now, see if they can go over each of the scenes again just for you."

"You're an absolute legend. Thanks, Lorraine."

CHAPTER 27

T he rest of the morning consisted of Sara rushing in and out of her office, checking on the progress Carla was making with regards to Matthew Lindon and answering the calls coming in from the appeal.

DCI Price dropped into the incident room around midday. Sara took her into her office and brought her up to date on things.

"That's great news. We need to make sure everything is airtight before we pick him up for questioning."

"I know that, ma'am. I've got a couple of men sitting outside his property—he won't go anywhere without us being on his tail."

"Let's hope the lab comes up trumps soon. I hate to say this when you're so close, but the super has been onto me about the number of murders we have on our hands at present. He's getting antsy and has urged me to urge you to try and hurry things along."

Sara fell back in her chair. "Jesus! What does he expect from us? We're doing our best in the circumstances. The first case only came to our attention at the beginning of last week. My team and I have worked our butts off in that time, attending scenes in the dead of the night— sorry, not the best choice of words. I'd like to think our efforts were more appreciated than they appear to be right now, ma'am."

DCI Price held her hands up in front of her. "Hey, you've got no complaints from me. I gave him an earful, don't you worry." She rose from her chair and smiled. "Carry on doing what you're doing. Give me a shout if I can lend a hand on anything, not that you don't appear to have everything under control anyway."

"A quick heads-up, my cat was at the vet's overnight."

DCI Price frowned. "Everything all right?"

Sara shrugged. "She appears to be better this morning, but she was poisoned. I'm not telling you because I want to use it as an excuse. I'm just stating facts."

"Damn, I'm sorry to hear that. Perhaps she picked up something from the site you're living on."

"I rang the site manager, and he told me there is nothing toxic on-site Misty could have got at."

"Are you thinking this was a deliberate act?"

"It seems that way, ma'am. Whoever did it will need police protection when I get hold of them."

"Is Misty all right now?"

"Yes, for now. The vet is monitoring her."

"Glad to hear it. Ring me if you need me, for anything, you hear me?"

"I will. Thanks, ma'am."

DCI Price left the room. As soon as Sara picked up a letter that needed her urgent response, her landline rang. "Hello. DI Ramsey."

"Sorry to trouble you, ma'am, it's Jeff."

Sara's attention was instantly gripped. The desk sergeant usually only contacted her when there was something wrong. "What is it, Sergeant?"

"One of my lads just brought something to my attention, and I thought you might be interested, ma'am."

"I'm listening. Do you want me to come down?"

"Maybe that would be for the best, ma'am. Or I could come up to see you?"

"My office is closing in on me today. I'll be there in a jiffy." Sara rushed around the desk and down the stairs to the reception area. "What have you got, Jeff?"

He motioned for her to step behind the counter and into the privacy of his back office. Lying on the desk was a black bag.

"I don't understand. What am I looking at, Sergeant?"

"My lads stopped off for a late breakfast up at Dinmore woods. Someone pointed out this bag and complained that people should be shot for dumping their rubbish in such a beautiful area."

"I agree with them. Shame on anyone dumping rubbish around here."

"My guys took the liberty of opening the bag rather than just dumping it in the bin, hoping the contents would lead back to the culprit. They'd then go round there and read them the riot act. Anyway, when they searched through the contents, something struck a chord with one of the lads." He pulled on a pair of latex gloves and then plucked an envelope out of the bag and showed it to her.

"Laurence Haldon? What the heck?" Sara searched her pocket and withdrew a blue glove of her own then riffled through the bag herself. "My God, this is all the paperwork that went missing from the Haldons' residence. I'm going to rush it over to the lab, see if they can pick up any fingerprints or DNA from it. Give your lads a pat on the back from me, Sergeant."

He beamed. "Will do, ma'am."

Sara tied a knot in the bag and raced out of the station. On the way to the car, she dialled Carla's mobile. "It's me. Something has come up. I'm on my way to the lab. I'll fill you in when I get back."

"Sounds intriguing. Thanks for letting me know; I wondered why you rushed out of here."

Sara tore through the lab and into Lorraine's office. She could see her in the locker room down the hall and gave her the thumbs-up. Lorraine gestured she would be two minutes. Sara paced the office until the pathologist entered the room.

"Something wrong? I hope you're not expecting the results fr… what's this?" she asked, pointing at the bag sitting on her desk.

"Remember the Haldons' daughter told me that her parents' personal file was missing?"

Lorraine shrugged. "I can't recall you telling me that, but go on."

"These are all the contents of the file. I need your guys to go over them. If we can match any fingerprints found to any other DNA or evidence we have, then we can nail the bastard."

"In this instance, *if* might be a very large word. Has anyone else touched the contents?"

"I don't think so. Do your best for me. I don't have to tell you how important this is."

"You're right, you don't. Leave it with me. I'll ring you ASAP." Lorraine picked up the bag and walked up the hallway while Sara took off in the other direction and drove back to the station.

CHAPTER 28

I t was a couple of fraught days before they received any definitive news they could use. The team had taken it in turns to keep Lindon under surveillance in that time. He'd ventured out once to go to the supermarket and returned home immediately. They had hoped he would leave the property at night, enabling them to catch him red-handed at another victim's house. No such luck, which Sara had mixed feelings about—she dreaded the thought of him attempting to kill someone else.

The call from Lorraine came at eleven on Thursday of that week. Sara's heart pumped faster during the conversation. "It's definitely him?"

"Yes, you're probably aware he was in trouble for a minor affray offence, so we had his fingerprints on file. The partial we took off the suitcase was a match. We also have his prints on a few sheets of paper from the bag you brought to my attention a few days ago. I'd say he's your culprit."

"Thanks, Lorraine. Can you email me the reports? I'll get on to the CPS, see if they'll accept that it's enough to make the arrest."

"I'm hitting the send button now."

While she waited for the email to ping in her inbox, she raced into the incident room to inform the team. "We've got him. Carla, get on to Craig, tell him to keep Lindon under surveillance for the rest of the day until I can organise the arrest." She punched the air with joy and relief.

CHAPTER 29

With the all-clear to make the arrest sanctioned, Sara and Carla joined up with armed police at Lindon's residence. They hit the house early, at six a.m. on the Friday of that week. Lindon was still in bed when they broke in. He left his bed in a daze, wearing only a pair of boxer shorts. Sara read him his rights and informed him why he was being arrested. She expected to hear some form of denial, but instead he grinned at her like the proverbial Cheshire cat. She was tempted to jab him in the stomach and his eyes but somehow resisted the urge to cause the man serious damage.

He was instructed to get dressed and taken to the station in the back of a secure police van. Sara decided to leave him to stew in a cell until just after lunch. "Are you ready for this?" she asked Carla.

"Yep, I can't wait to see you tear him apart."

Sara laughed. "Feel free to join in the fun at any time."

"Nope, you deserve to handle this one all by yourself."

"We'll see."

They made their way down the stairs and told the desk sergeant they were ready to interview Lindon.

"I'll send him in, ma'am. His brief is here." He motioned over to the seats in the waiting room, to a young suited gentleman.

"Hello, sir. I don't know you, do I?"

"Charles Darley at your service. My client rang me this morning. I hope you're sure it's him, Inspector?"

"I am. Walk this way, and we'll get settled."

Sitting in the interview room, Sara felt anxious, more anxious than normal for some unknown reason.

Lindon walked arrogantly into the room a few moments later, accompanied by a heavy-set PC.

Carla said the usual verbiage for the tape before Sara took over. "Hello again, Matthew. You're aware of the charges we're bringing against you. Do you have anything to say regarding those charges?"

"No comment."

Sara had a feeling he would probably go down this route. Most criminals who had a lot of evidence against them did the same. "I'm not going to beat around the bush here, I have better things to do with my valuable time. We can place you at the scene of Tina Haldon's murder and that of your girlfriend, Dawn Dawson. There's no point denying it. Also, we can link you to the first murder that took place out in Bodenham, that of Ted and Maureen Flowers, whom you were related to through marriage, I believe, at one time. What I want to know is, why? Why kill these innocent people in such a short space of time?"

He folded his arms and stared at Sara. She searched deep into his large brown eyes, seeking answers and found nothing.

He grinned broadly and said, "No comment."

"This interview is now ended. Thank you, Mr Darley, for attending. Sorry you felt the need to advise your client to go down the 'no comment' route. All it does is highlight his guilt. We've taken your car in to be examined, Mr Lindon."

Lindon's eyebrow raised, and then his eyes narrowed. Sara had a feeling they were about to discover something of importance inside the vehicle, judging by his reaction.

"Take Mr Lindon back to his cell, Constable."

They followed Lindon out the room.

Sara bid the solicitor farewell and returned to the incident room with Carla. "Did you gauge his reaction when I mentioned his car?"

"I did."

"Hopefully, we'll get some news on that either today or tomorrow."

Sara left work, feeling a huge weight had been lifted from her shoulders. Misty wrapped herself around her legs the minute she stepped into the house. She sighed, happy that things had returned to normal. Thinking her achievements needed celebrating, she took a bottle of wine from the fridge and opened it, then she withdrew a piece of steak she had been saving from the freezer and placed it in the microwave to defrost while she chopped up a few onions, peeled some mushrooms and scrubbed a potato ready to bake in its jacket. This would be the first proper meal she had cooked for herself in over a week, and she intended to enjoy it.

After her meal was cooked, eaten and she'd cleared up the kitchen, she took the rest of her wine through to the lounge to catch up on her favourite series, *Shades of Blue*. Halfway through the episode, her phone tinkled. She read the text message, unsure how she should feel. It was from Donald.

Hi, Sara, it's been a while since we've chatted. Give me a ring when you have the chance. Donald x

Stroking Misty, she asked, "What do you think, girl? Should we give him a chance?" Misty ignored her and curled up into a ball. "Thanks, that's a great help."

EPILOGUE

A few days later, once the forensic reports were to hand, Sara brought DCI Price up to date. "Here's where we stand, ma'am. It has now been confirmed that Matthew Lindon was responsible for all six murders. I had another brief chat with him late yesterday afternoon. He admitted on tape that he killed his girlfriend, Dawn. What he actually said was that when the loan shark he owed a significant amount of money to told his heavies to beat him up, he then took his anger out on Dawn and went too far."

"Nice. Are you saying that she didn't actually do anything wrong?" DCI Price shook her head in disgust.

"That's exactly what I'm saying, ma'am. It just goes to show what little value a person's life has to some people, doesn't it?"

"You're not wrong. What about the other murders? How have you tied him to those?"

"Forensics found the knife he used tucked under the passenger seat of his car. They also found an address book, possibly the one missing from the Flowers' residence. The other victims' names were circled. They also removed clothes he'd worn in the past few days from his bedroom and examined them. They revealed large amounts of blood spatter. The analysis is ongoing. To date, they've been able to attribute at least three of the victims' blood to the garments."

"What about the bloody footprint at the first scene? See, I do listen."

Sara smiled. "I know you do. Yes, that was the easiest item forensics had to match."

"What a bastard. And it was all about the money? Because he got into debt and had no way of paying it off?" DCI Price shook her head again. "What a despicable creature. I know I shouldn't say this, but I hope he gets what's coming to him on the inside."

"My thoughts precisely, ma'am. I know he took a hammering from the loan shark's men, he's still showing signs of heavy bruising; however, he didn't actually receive any broken bones. I'd like to see that alter once he gets inside. One last thing, when they searched his house they found a large area of blood that he'd tried to wipe up in the kitchen. That blood belonged to Dawn, so even if he hadn't admitted to killing her, we would have had him bang to rights on that evidence."

"I'm glad you and your team caught him. Wait! What about your cat? Was he behind that, too?"

Sara tutted. "I questioned him about that, and he flat-out denied he was responsible. I'm inclined to think he's innocent on that, ma'am, but who knows?"

The DCI seemed shocked to learn the news. "My God, seriously? So who do you think is responsible for that?"

Sara shrugged. "I'm still investigating that. Maybe I'll keep a closer eye on my neighbours. Perhaps one of them took a dislike to Misty weeing in their garden. Hard to believe, but you just never know these days."

"I hope you find the culprit soon. Is your pussy fully recovered now?" the DCI asked with a twinkle in her eye.

Sara chuckled. "Yes, my pussy is in full working order again you'll be pleased to know, ma'am."

"Another case or cases solved efficiently and in a timely manner, for which we're all appreciative, Inspector. You should all give yourselves a pat on the back."

"We aim to please. Right, I better get on, ma'am. I said I'd keep all the relatives involved with what was going on."

"That's decent of you. Before you go, what about the victim who is in ICU? Any news on him?"

"Sorry, yes. He regained consciousness late yesterday afternoon. I rushed over to see him. He was able to formally identify Lindon as the killer. The poor man is beside himself, feels guilty for not being able to save his wife."

"I bet he does. Very sad indeed. Let's hope that guilt doesn't hamper his recovery."

"If I'm honest with you, I fear it might."

"That poor man. I sometimes wonder if in cases such as this the victim wouldn't be better off dead. I know that sounds harsh, however, look at the alternative. He's going to be forced to live in that house, knowing that his wife was murdered in front of his eyes and that he was unable to protect her... Shit! I'm sorry, I didn't mean...just ignore me."

"It's okay, ma'am. Mr Haldon's experience was slightly different to mine. My own recovery is going well; there's no need for anyone to tiptoe around me when something such as this is highlighted. We all have our crosses to bear in life."

"We do. You're a very special person, Sara. You know where I am if ever things get on top of you, right?"

"I know. Thank you, ma'am." Sara left the DCI's office and swiped away a stray tear that caught her out. She went back to her desk and spent the next hour or so ringing the family members, bringing them up to date with the good news about Matthew Lindon. They were all shocked to learn of his arrest and his involvement in the crimes after the Flowers family had welcomed him into the fold.

After work, the team had a quiet drink at the local pub to celebrate the closure of one of their toughest cases to date. Sara only stopped for the one drink—she was super eager to get home to see how Misty was.

She'd not long stepped through the front door when her mobile rang. She flopped onto the couch, planted Misty on her lap then answered the call. "Hello." She had trouble recognising the number on the caller ID.

"Hi, Mrs Ramsey, it's Mark Fisher. The vet calling to see how Misty is?"

"Oh, hi, Dr Fisher. I've just this second got home. She's purring away on my lap and seems fine. Thank you so much for ringing, it's very kind of you."

"Not at all. By the way, it's Mark, I hate to be formal with my clients."

Sara sniggered. "That's a deal. I'm Sara in that case."

He cleared his throat and then said, "I was wondering if you'd consider going out for a drink with me in the future, Sara. Sorry if that sounds a bit forward of me to suggest such a thing when we've only just met."

Sara was taken aback for a moment or two and struggled to find the words to respond, prompting him to ask, "Are you still there? Sorry, it's okay for you to say no, I shouldn't have asked."

"No, wait. I'm sorry, you took me by surprise, that's all. Okay, why not?"

"Are you sure? Don't feel obliged or forced into a corner. I have broad shoulders and I'm used to rejection."

Sara laughed. "Really? No, it's fine, honestly. I'd love to come for a drink with you."

"What about Saturday?"

"Sounds perfect."

"I'll pick you up. I have your address on file. Look forward to seeing you at eight o'clock, will that do?"

"See you at eight. Thank you, Mark."

"No, thank you. See you on Saturday."

Sara ended the call and went through to the kitchen to see what was sitting in the fridge for dinner. On the way, she caught a glimpse of herself in the hall mirror. She was utterly beaming, and for the first time in ages her heart felt lighter.

After feeding Misty and letting her out into the garden, she knocked up a stir-fry for herself and collapsed on the couch to watch the evening news. Halfway through her meal, her phone rang again, and she angled the mobile to see the screen. *Bloody hell, Donald again. What is his problem? Maybe I should tell him I have a date on Saturday. Maybe not.* "Hi, Donald. I'm eating dinner. What can I do for you?"

"Anything nice?"

"Liver stir-fry, one of my favourites."

"Yuck, can't stand liver. Busy day at work?"

"Very. You?"

"Hit and miss. Any chance we can have dinner this week?"

Sara rolled her eyes, thankful that he wasn't in the room with her. "Not this week. I have a ton of paperwork ahead of me over the next few days. It goes with the territory when we crack a case."

"You solved the case of the murders?"

"That's right."

"Excellent news, you are clever."

"Teamwork. I'm nothing special. Anyway, must fly, my dinner is getting cold. Oh, your mum rang, by the way. I'll try and nip over to see you all in the next few weeks, work permitting."

"Great. I can't wait to see you again, it's been a long time, Sara. Enjoy your meal."

"Thanks." She ended the call and finished her stir-fry then went through to the kitchen to wash up. When she returned with a cup of coffee and a custard cream in her hand, she noticed the screen on her phone was lit up, signifying she'd missed a text. After punching in her password, she scrolled through to her text messages.

Your cat was lucky. It was a warning. Next time it'll be you who needs hospitalisation!

S ara stared at the screen, gobsmacked. *Who? Why?*

She tried to ring the number, but the call remained unanswered. Her hand was shaking uncontrollably. She flew around the house to ensure all the windows and doors were shut and locked.

If it wasn't Lindon who'd poisoned Misty, then who was it?

THE END

LETTER TO YOU, THE READER.

Dear Reader,

thank you for coming on this emotional journey with my newest detective DI Sara Ramsey. There will be more investigations for her to solve in the future, I promise.

In the meantime, why not try one of my other series? The series that started them all, the bestselling Justice series.

You can read the first chapter here:

Cruel Justice

Thank you for supporting my work.

M A Comley

P.S. Reviews are like cupcakes to authors, won't you consider leaving one today? We love cupcakes.

KEEP IN TOUCH WITH M A COMLEY

Twitter
https://twitter.com/Melcom1

Blog
http://melcomley.blogspot.com

Facebook
http://smarturl.it/sps7jh

Newsletter
http://smarturl.it/8jtcvv

BookBub
www.bookbub.com/authors/m-a-comley

ABOUT THE AUTHOR

M A Comley is a New York Times and USA Today bestselling author of crime fiction. To date (November 2018) she has over 80 titles published.

Her books have reached the top of the charts on all platforms in ebook format, Top 20 on Amazon, Top 5 on iTunes, number 2 on Barnes and Noble and Top 5 on KOBO. She has sold over two and a half million copies worldwide.

In her spare time, she doesn't tend to get much, she enjoys spending time walking her dog in rural Herefordshire, UK.

Her love of reading and specifically the devious minds of killers is what led her to pen her first book in the genre she adores.

Look out for more books coming in the future in the cozy mystery genre.

facebook.com/Mel-Comley-264745836884860

twitter.com/Melcom1

bookbub.com/authors/m-a-comley

12877860R00129

Printed in Great Britain
by Amazon